THE BOBBSEY TWINS'
SEARCH IN THE GREAT CITY

Above them all, the towering Statue of Liberty
gazed down serenely

The Bobbsey Twins' Search in the Great City

By

LAURA LEE HOPE

GROSSET & DUNLAP
Publishers • New York

Published in 2004 by Grosset & Dunlap, a division of Penguin Young
Readers Group, 345 Hudson Street, New York, New York 10014.
GROSSET & DUNLAP is a trademark of Penguin Group (USA) Inc.
THE BOBBSEY TWINS® is a registered trademark of
Simon & Schuster, Inc.

Printed in the U.S.A.

ISBN 0-448-43760-0

1 3 5 7 9 10 8 6 4 2

CONTENTS

CHAPTER I

MYSTERIOUS FOOTPRINTS

"HURRAY!" Freddie Bobbsey shouted as he turned a double somersault on the grass. "We're going on a picnic!"

"Yes, and Dinah's making a blueberry pie for us to take along," his sister Flossie told him.

Freddie and Flossie were six-year-old twins. Both had chubby faces, blond curls, and impish blue eyes.

A twelve-year-old boy with brown hair and eyes came around the corner of the Bobbseys' comfortable, rambling house. He was Bert Bobbsey, their brother. With him was Snap, the family pet, a beautiful shaggy white dog.

"Snap's going on the picnic with us," Bert announced. "Dad says he can ride in the back of the station wagon with the picnic baskets."

"Ooo, I hope he won't eat the pie!" Freddie put in, looking worried.

1

"Where are we going for our picnic, Bert?" Flossie asked.

Bert did not know, but his twin sister who came out of the house answered the question. Nan was slim, dark too, and very pretty. "We're going to drive to the Meredith estate, and Daddy says he knows a good spot where we can eat our lunch on the way."

"What's the Meredith 'state?" Flossie questioned, her blue eyes round.

Nan explained that Mr. Meredith had died recently and left his large house and grounds, which were directly across Lake Metoka from the Bobbseys' house, to the county for a public park. "There's a small zoo in it," she added.

"I hope they have lots of lions and bears and tigers and—" Freddie paused, out of breath.

Mr. and Mrs. Bobbsey appeared in the kitchen doorway. "Come on, children. Get your sweaters," their mother called. She was slender and dark-haired. Nan and Bert looked a great deal like her.

"The Bobbsey expedition is about to start!" Mr. Bobbsey said smiling, as he and Bert lifted the picnic baskets into the back of the station wagon.

Snap wagged his tail and jumped in while Bert held the door open for him. Just then Dinah, the jolly woman who helped Mrs.

Bobbsey with the cooking, came running out of the house.

"Don't forget this here pie," she called.

"It looks delicious, Dinah," Mrs. Bobbsey complimented the cook.

"I sure hope it tastes good." Then, Dinah added, "Don't you all lose my pie pan. I'm mighty partial to this special one!"

"We'll bring it back, Dinah," Nan assured her. "But not with any pie in it!"

Everyone laughed as they climbed into the car, and soon they were riding along the shore road. Lake Metoka was blue and sparkling in the June sunshine.

"Oh, aren't picnics fun?" Nan cried. "And it's wonderful to go on one the first day of vacation!"

Mrs. Bobbsey turned around and smiled at her daughter. "Your father has a plan for us all which will be even more fun than the picnic," she said.

"Oh, what is it, Daddy?" Flossie asked eagerly.

"Yes, please tell us!" the others chorused.

Mr. Bobbsey laughed. "Calm down, all of you! I think I may have to go to New York on business," he explained. "Your mother and I have decided that it would be nice for the whole family to make a trip together to the big city."

Mr. Bobbsey owned a lumberyard in Lakeport and often traveled on business. In this way the twins had visited many places and had numerous adventures.

"I won't know definitely," the twins' father continued, "until I hear from Mr. Hanks who is to phone me this afternoon at five."

"A trip would be great!" Bert exclaimed. "We'd sure have a wonderful time in New York." The other children agreed enthusiastically.

Flossie, looking out the window, asked suddenly, "Why are we going away from the lake, Daddy?"

The road turned toward the west at this point and joined another highway about a mile beyond. Mr. Bobbsey explained this and then added, "We'll turn onto an old road that crosses the highway soon. It follows the lake shore most of the way, and there are woods where we can have our lunch."

"Goody!" exclaimed Flossie. "I see some trees over there."

"And here's the road," said her father, leaving the highway. He drove along the lake for a while and then stopped at the edge of a lovely grove.

"Oh, picnic tables and fireplaces," Nan exclaimed. "Isn't it almost time for lunch?"

"It's twelve o'clock on the nose," Bert said, looking at his watch. "And I could eat a horse!"

Mr. Bobbsey parked the car at the side of the road and the children carried the baskets to a nearby table. Freddie and Flossie ran around inspecting the grove.

"There's a path that goes down to the lake," Freddie announced as he took his place at the table. "May I go down as soon as I eat my chicken and sandwiches? I'd like to have my pie after I take a little walk."

"Me, too," Flossie said, biting into her sandwich. "We can run down to the lake and back again to get more hungry for the pie."

"All right, dear," Mrs. Bobbsey said. "But don't stay long if you want to go to the Meredith place."

As soon as they had finished the first part of their lunch, the younger twins asked to be excused. Then they set off down the path with Snap at their heels.

The others were about to have their dessert when they heard Freddie shout, "Mother! Daddy! Come look! There's some great big footprints in the sand!" He appeared on the path with Flossie, with Snap close behind him.

"They're like my kitty's footmarks, only BIG!" Flossie told the family excitedly.

"This I must see," said Bert, jumping up.

Nan followed and so did Mr. Bobbsey. Mrs. Bobbsey had started to cut the pie, so she waited to slip it into its cellophane cover before she, too, went down the path.

She found the others looking at the strange

marks in the wet sand. They appeared to be footprints of a very large cat.

"How queer!" exclaimed Bert. "Are there
wildcats around here, Dad?"

Mr. Bobbsey had lived in this section of the
country since he was a boy. He shook his head.
"I've never heard of wildcats or bobcats in these
woods," he said in a puzzled voice.

"Could it be an animal from the zoo?" Nan asked. "Maybe the Meredith zoo?"

"Perhaps it's the tiger that Freddie wanted to see," suggested Bert teasingly.

"I don't want to see it now," Freddie said, looking at the huge tracks. "Let's go to the car, Daddy."

"Whatever it was," said his father as they went back up the path, "it was traveling east."

Nan had gone on ahead and the family was startled to hear her give a sharp "OH!" As they hurried toward her, Nan cried out, "THE PIE IS GONE!"

The Bobbseys stared in amazement at the table.

"Who could have taken it?" asked Mrs. Bobbsey. "It was here a minute ago!"

"Could the animal have knocked it off the table?" asked Bert, looking around the ground.

"Daddy, if it was a very smart tiger from a zoo, could it carry a pie away?" Freddie asked in a small voice.

"No, son," Mr. Bobbsey answered. "I'm sure this thief had hands." He walked to the edge of the grove to look down the road. "I also think he had wheels," he continued as he came back to the picnic table. "There's a cloud of dust down the road which means that a car passed here recently. While we were down at the lake looking at the tracks, someone driving by must have seen Dinah's pie. It wouldn't take a minute to hop out and grab it."

"Oh dear! That was Dinah's favorite pie pan," moaned Nan. "And I promised we'd bring it back."

"I hope the pie stealer meets the man-eating tiger," growled Bert. "I wanted some of that good blueberry pie!"

"We may as well drive on to the Meredith estate," Mr. Bobbsey said. "Remember, I must be home by five to get the New York call."

They all piled into the station wagon, with Snap again in the rear. The mention of New York had put the missing pie out of the minds of the twins for the moment.

"If we do go to New York, how long will we stay, Dad?" Bert asked.

"I think I can finish my business in a few days, but we'll plan to stay about a week," his father answered. "There are many things I want you to see while we're there."

"Whoops! A whole week in New York!" exclaimed Freddie. "Is there a zoo?"

"Oh yes. A wonderful zoo," his mother said. "I've been there many times."

The Bobbsey car had been traveling at a good

pace and now overtook another one on the road.

"Daddy, do you think this is the pie stealer's car?" Freddie asked.

A familiar face appeared in the window of the other automobile as they passed it. "See the wonderful Bobbsey twins!" a voice jeered. "They're going to be on exhibit at the new zoo!"

"That's Danny Rugg in his uncle's car!" Nan exclaimed. "I'll bet he took our pie!"

Danny Rugg was a boy about Bert's age. He was in Bert's class at school and, being somewhat of a bully, was always making trouble for the Bobbsey children.

"Well, if Danny did take the pie," Nan said, "we'll have a hard time getting Dinah's plate back."

Mr. Bobbsey by now had left the car with Danny in it far behind. The road turned along the lake again.

Suddenly Bert leaned from the window, "Look!" he cried, "Here are the big tracks again in the wet sand!"

Mr. Bobbsey stopped the car and they all alighted to examine the footprints. Snap, left in the station wagon, whined to get out.

Bert followed the tracks along the shore, then turned and hurried back. "The footprints stop down the beach a little ways," he said. "Where do you think the animal went from here?"

Mr. Bobbsey looked across the road to the grove. "Back in the car, everybody," he called. "We won't take any chances. The animal may be there in the woods."

As the rest hurried toward the station wagon, Mr. Bobbsey took Flossie by the hand. In her excitement the little girl lost her shoe.

Bert bent to pick it up. Just then Snap's whines turned to sharp, high barks. Bert looked back. Running out of the grove and heading straight for him was a large catlike animal!

CHAPTER II

A RUNAWAY CHEETAH

"HURRY, Bert!" Nan cried frantically as she held the car door open for her brother.

A moment later he reached the car and jumped inside. Nan slammed the door while the small twins and their parents hurriedly rolled up the windows. Then everyone sighed with relief.

"Oh, thank goodness you're safe, son!" Mrs. Bobbsey exclaimed. "That was a narrow escape!"

"Wha—what kind of animal is it?" Bert asked, when he had caught his breath.

"A cheetah," Mr. Bobbsey replied, adding that it was a member of the leopard family.

The cheetah did indeed very much resemble the long, slender-limbed leopard. Its head was small in proportion to its three-foot height and Bert guessed that the beast was about five feet long, not counting its tail.

Mr. Bobbsey pointed out the cheetah's rather rough looking, deep fawn-colored fur. The spots on it were small and solid in contrast to the leopard's circular markings.

"I've seen cheetahs in zoos and at the circus," Nan spoke up. "But I can't understand what this one's doing around here!"

"He must have escaped from a traveling-circus van," Bert deduced. "Dad, I think we should notify the authorities in Lakeport that he is loose."

"I agree," Mr. Bobbsey said, and started the engine.

As the car rolled forward, the cheetah bounded ahead. The animal waited until he was abreast with the right fender, then made a graceful leap over the hood.

Screech! Mr. Bobbsey applied the brakes as the small twins, no longer frightened, howled with laughter.

"He's a playful cheetah!" Flossie giggled.

"We'll have to teach Snoop that trick," her twin said, referring to the family's cat.

Mr. Bobbsey chuckled. "Well I can't drive with that crazy animal playing leapfrog over the car!" he exclaimed.

At that moment they saw a small truck coming down the road toward them. The cheetah, with lightning speed, bounded fifteen feet ahead, then stopped and stretched out lazily in the center of the road.

"He's going to be hit!" Flossie cried out.

But such was not the case, for just then the truck careened to a stop directly beside the tawny animal. A man got out of the driver's seat and walked toward the beast.

"Here Rajah! Be a good boy!" the Bobbseys heard him say. In his outstretched hand the man held three frankfurters.

The cheetah gulped the food, then licked the man's hand as gently as a kitten. The driver returned to the truck for a large collar, which he snapped about the cheetah's neck. When this was done he led the animal to the back of the truck, opened a door, and shut him inside.

The man now walked over to speak to the amazed Bobbseys. "Well folks, I guess you were scared when you saw Rajah here. He looks fierce but he's as tame as a kitten, if you just give him something to eat."

Mr. Bobbsey introduced himself and his family, and the man said his name was Joe Monk.

Nan told what had happened, then asked, "Where did Rajah come from?"

"The Meredith zoo," the man replied. "One of our helpers forgot to lock the cage door last night. Rajah's mighty clever and he somehow turned the door handle. There's a break in the high wire fence around the place. He must have gone through there and headed for the woods."

"Does he run away often?" Freddie asked worriedly.

The man smiled. "No, this is the first time. And it won't happen again. The fence will be mended today."

"Is the zoo open to visitors?" Mrs. Bobbsey asked. "We're on our way to the estate."

"Well, not officially," Mr. Monk said, "but I'll be glad to show you around if you want to follow me."

The Bobbseys eagerly accepted the invitation. After the man had turned his truck around, they followed close behind him. A few miles farther on, the truck turned onto the highway going east. Along one side ran a high brick wall.

"This wall encloses the Meredith estate," Mr. Bobbsey explained.

In a few minutes Mr. Monk turned into a driveway and stopped at a gate. It was set in a high fence made of narrow wooden palings with curved wire netting on top.

"I can see how hard it would be for an animal to get out of this place," said Bert. "Look, they're mending the fence over there."

The truck stopped and the driver came back to speak to the Bobbseys. "You'd better park here," he said. "You'll have to leave the dog in the car. Go inside, and I'll join you as soon as I put Rajah back in his cage."

When the Bobbseys walked toward the gate, it was opened at once by a guard who greeted them pleasantly. As they entered, they could see a group of low brick buildings set around a flagstone terrace. There was a green-tiled pool in the center and about it were grouped aluminum chairs and tables.

"Is this a zoo?" Freddie asked, puzzled.

Flossie ran to look into the pool. "Oh what a bee-yoo-ti-ful fish!" she exclaimed. "They're all colors and some have wings."

"Those aren't wings, Flossie. They're fins," Nan said. "These must be angel fish."

"Good morning," said a voice as a man stepped onto the terrace. "I'm Bob Hunt, keeper of this zoo. May I show you around?"

Mr. Bobbsey introduced his family and himself. "This is an amazing place," he said as they went toward the buildings.

"It is," Mr. Hunt agreed. "Over there to the right of the last building is the bear pit." He pointed to a tall tree with a moat around it. "During the summer the bears are out there. Then, to the left of the first brick building there is the monkeys' summer home. They haven't gone out yet as it's still a little early."

The man led the Bobbseys into the first of the buildings. It was cool and fresh smelling. The walls and floor were colored the soft green of forest trees.

"What lovely tiles!" exclaimed Mrs. Bobbsey. "And how spotlessly clean the place is!"

A row of empty cages lined one wall, but as Mrs. Bobbsey spoke a lion came softly into one from an opening in the back.

"The animals are in the outdoor cages this morning, but they will come inside if they hear visitors." The keeper laughed. "They love company."

"Oh there's Rajah!" exclaimed Bert, as two cheetahs appeared in one of the cages. He went over to speak to them.

Nan and Flossie wandered along and presently Flossie called out, "Daddy, here is the man-eating tiger!"

"That's Ranee," Mr. Hunt told her. "She was

a tiny cub when we got her. My wife fed her from a bottle."

The children stared at the great black-striped creature, lying on the ledge above their heads.

"Is she tame like the cheetahs?" asked Nan.

Mr. Hunt shook his head. "I wouldn't trust her too far," he said, "although my wife isn't afraid to enter her cage if necessary."

A bell tinkled out in the yard. Mr. Hunt turned to say to the twins, "That is the ice cream man. Would you like cones, children? It was the habit of Mr. Meredith to give them to children who were his guests at the zoo, and we're continuing it."

"How kind!" exclaimed Mrs. Bobbsey.

The twins thanked Mr. Hunt and ran outside to the terrace where the ice cream vendor was standing with his little cart.

When they returned with their ice cream cones Mr. Hunt and their parents had gone on into the next building. The driver of the truck followed the twins in and tossed a cone into Rajah's cage. The cheetah ran to taste it and then pushed it away with his paw.

"Are all the animals here tame?" asked Freddie.

"Not all of them," the keeper replied. "But you must be sure to visit the monkeys' house. They are so tame that they play like children."

As the twins continued to watch the cheetahs, the man waved good-by and walked on into the next building. Suddenly something landed on Bert's back with such force that he almost fell down. A thin hairy arm shot over his shoulder and snatched the cone from his hand.

"A monkey!" Nan gasped. "Where did it come from?"

Flossie turned in time to see Danny Rugg tiptoeing out of the room. He was doubled up with laughter.

The monkey had jumped to the floor and was

gobbling the cone and chattering in shrill tones. Bert rubbed his neck in a bewildered way.

"Danny brought it!" Flossie cried. "I saw him sneaking out the door just now!"

"I'll fix that pie stealer!" Bert exclaimed and started for the door. Freddie ran along beside him, and the girls followed. They found Danny standing beside his uncle on the terrace.

"You're full of tricks today, Danny," Bert said scornfully, "but you'll have to return the pie pan."

"You're crazy!" the bully said defiantly. "I haven't got any old pie pan!"

"Didn't you snatch a blueberry pie from our picnic table this morning?" Bert asked severely.

"No!" Danny shouted angrily.

"I can vouch for that, Bert." Danny's uncle spoke up. "Danny has been with me all morning."

"I'm sorry, sir," Bert apologized. "We passed your car and I thought—"

"Of course you blamed me," Danny finished Bert's sentence rudely.

Bert turned away and the twins walked out onto the terrace where their parents were talking with Mr. Hunt.

"I've been hearing about your meeting with Rajah this morning," the zoo keeper said to Bert. "I'm sorry you had such a fright. Rajah is harmless, but of course you didn't know that."

"I figured he'd come home when he got tired, but I sent a truck after him so he wouldn't be scaring a lot of people," Mr. Hunt continued.

At that moment a low rumble of thunder sounded and the sun disappeared under a mass of blue-black clouds.

"We should start for home," said Mr. Bobbsey. "I must be in Lakeport by five o'clock. Thank you for letting us look around."

"You'd better take the short cut," Mr. Hunt advised. "Turn right at the brick wall and go to the open gate at the end. Drive through to the end of that road and you'll see another open gate. Just outside that is Route 7 which will get you into Lakeport in fifteen minutes."

"That will be a great help," Mr. Bobbsey said. "We'll have to see the bear pit another time."

When the Bobbseys reached their car Snap greeted them excitedly, then settled down. As they left the driveway, the rain came down in torrents.

Mr. Bobbsey turned at the corner of the wall and in a few minutes said, "Here's the open gate. I didn't expect it so soon." He drove through into a deep woods.

"There's a car ahead of us," Flossie exclaimed, as a shabby automobile appeared in the dim light.

"This must be the right road then," said her father. He switched on the headlights, because the storm had made the woods very dark.

"It's gone!" Flossie cried. "The car's gone!"

"There's probably a turn in the road," Mrs. Bobbsey observed as they drove along slowly. "It couldn't just disappear."

"Boy, what big trees!" Bert exclaimed. "It seems a million miles from nowhere in here."

Suddenly the Bobbsey car swerved as the headlights showed a turn in the road. The next moment there was a terrific jolt as the front wheels of the station wagon sank into a deep hole!

CHAPTER III

FACE IN THE WINDOW

FOR a moment the Bobbseys were too shaken to speak. Then Mr. Bobbsey looked around and asked, "Is everybody all right?"

"Yes," the twins answered together, and Mrs. Bobbsey said she was not hurt.

Mr. Bobbsey raced the motor as he tried to back out of the ditch. But the hole was deep, and the wheels only spun around.

"What'll we do, Dad?" Bert asked.

"Shall I get out and push the car?" Freddie asked helpfully. "I'm awfully strong for my age."

His father smiled. "Thank you for offering, Freddie, but I'm afraid this job needs something stronger than all of us combined."

"Maybe Bert and I can find a garage," Nan suggested, "if we walk back to the highway." She started to get out of the car but Mr. Bobbsey stopped her. "There must be a house somewhere on this road and it will have a telephone," he said. "We'll wait until the storm lets up a little and then try to find a house."

It had grown very dark in the woods and—although the rain was checked somewhat by the dense canopy of leaves overhead—the downpour was steady. Lightning flashed and thunder cannonaded about them like giant bowling balls.

"Dad, why should there be a big hole like this in the middle of a road if it's used as a short cut to Route 7?" Nan asked.

Mr. Bobbsey turned to smile at her. "That's a good question, Nan. I think the answer is that this isn't the short cut. I'm afraid that I came through the wrong gate. This road doesn't look as if it's been used for some time."

"But, Dad, the man said to go in the first open gate," Bert protested.

"And," Flossie spoke up, "that other car came on this road too."

"So it did!" her father agreed. "I wonder where the car is now. It must have turned off or it would have hit this hole too."

"There wasn't any other road where it could have turned off," Bert said uneasily. "At least, I didn't see one."

The headlights made the rain resemble golden mist, and the woods looked mysterious. Flossie snuggled close to Nan. "It's sort of spooky, isn't it?" she murmured.

Nan laughed. "It's like the enchanted forest in a fairy tale," she said and leaned forward to look through the window. "Oh!" she exclaimed and drew back quickly.

Following her pointing finger Bert and Freddie saw a man standing close to the window. At

that moment there was a vivid flash of lightning. In the glare the children got a clear view of the stranger.

He had a scar on his left cheek and the lid of his left eye drooped oddly. His chin was covered with a purplish discoloration. On his tie clip was a horse's head with a flashing ruby eye.

The man looked so ugly and so desperate that Freddie and Nan shrank back, but Bert said quickly, "Here's a man, Dad. Perhaps he can help us."

Mr. and Mrs. Bobbsey and Flossie in the front seat had not seen the stranger, but Mr. Bobbsey rolled down his window at once. Before he could speak, the fellow had scrambled to the side of the road and disappeared into the high shrubbery. Another flash of lightning at this moment revealed a small bag in his hand. Then he was gone.

"That's strange," said Mrs. Bobbsey. "Why did he run away?"

Her husband opened the door and climbed out on the road. "Hello there!" he called. "Hello!"

No answer came. The twins watched the bushes anxiously, but no one emerged.

"The rain has let up a bit. I'll try to find a house," Mr. Bobbsey said.

He set off up the road. Snap growled and whined nervously.

"Quiet, boy," Bert said. "I'll bet you'd give that ugly character a scare if I let you out, but he might hurt you."

"Look!" Nan exclaimed a few minutes later. "Daddy has found someone."

A jolly-looking older man had come onto the road a few feet ahead of Mr. Bobbsey and was now talking to him. In a minute the two men came back to the car and Mr. Bobbsey opened the door.

"This is Mr. Jack Whipple, the caretaker of the Meredith estate," he told them. "Mr. Whipple has invited us to wait at his house until I can get someone to help us. He has a phone."

Mr. Whipple helped Mrs. Bobbsey to the road while the twins' father lifted Flossie and Freddie up.

"Bring your dog," the caretaker said to Bert. "You may have rather a long wait, because the garage in Berlin is always pretty busy."

Bert opened the back of the station wagon, and Snap jumped out, barking furiously. He ran at once toward the bushes where the man had disappeared.

"Snap! Come back here!" Bert ordered. The faithful dog obeyed unwillingly and followed them as they hurried along behind the caretaker.

It had started to rain hard again. The house was not far away, but tall trees and high shrubbery hid it from the road. A short path led to the brown shingled cottage which looked very cozy with its windows reflecting a flickering fire.

"I'm glad there's a fire," said Bert to his twin as they ran up on the porch. "I'm cold."

Snap shook himself before he went inside with the others. Then he ran straight to the hearth and stretched himself out comfortably.

Mr. Whipple laughed. "I hope you'll all make yourselves as much at home as Snap has." Then he turned to Mr. Bobbsey. "You say these are two pairs of twins?" he asked. "I'm very partial to twins, especially boy and girl twins. We had a pair in my own family. They were my younger brother and sister."

Flossie looked up into the man's twinkling brown eyes. "Where are they now?" she asked.

"I wish I knew, honey," was Mr. Whipple's surprising answer. Then he hurried off to show Mr. Bobbsey where the telephone was and gave him the number of the Berlin garage.

Mr. Whipple returned presently and drew up a chair beside the group by the fire. Flossie moved a little closer to him.

"Did your twins go away, Mr. Whipple?" she asked.

"Flossie dear," Mrs. Bobbsey protested, "don't ask so many questions."

The caretaker put out his hand and touched Flossie's golden curls. "I don't wonder that she asks," he said to Mrs. Bobbsey. "People don't often lose a family. It happened a long time ago when I was a boy of twelve and the twins were six years younger. We lived in a lumber camp in Oregon, and when our parents died some neighbors took the twins to live with them. I stayed to work in the camp. Meanwhile the people moved away, and I have never been able to find my brother and sister."

"What a sad story!" exclaimed Mrs. Bobbsey.

Nan and Bert were both thinking how awful it would be to lose Flossie and Freddie and they felt very sorry for Mr. Jack Whipple.

"Didn't the family tell you where they were going?" Nan asked him.

"I knew where they moved to first," he explained. "But the year I was fifteen the letters stopped coming. I left the camp and tried to find the twins. But they were not at the address I had, and none of the neighbors knew where they had gone!" Mr. Whipple sighed.

At that moment Mr. Bobbsey came in from the next room and sat down beside the group at the fire. "The line to the garage is busy," he said. "I'll try again in a little while."

"I've been wondering how you happened to be on that road," the caretaker said. "It hasn't been used for years."

"What made the big hole in it?" Freddie asked.

"There was an enormous boulder there," Mr. Whipple explained. "The rain washed out the road and left the stone exposed, so Mr. Meredith had it removed and the hole filled in. Some of the gardener's children must have been digging there and the soft earth caved in.

"That gate has been locked since the west wing

of the house was closed off and the drive wasn't used any more," he continued.

"The keeper at the zoo told me to turn at the first open gate to reach Route 7," Mr. Bobbsey told him. "I thought I was following instructions because that gate was open."

"It was?" the caretaker asked in surprise. "I can't understand that. The gate Mr. Hunt meant is nearly at the end of the west wall."

"Another car came through this one before we did," Freddie announced.

"Dad!" exclaimed Bert, struck by a sudden thought. "I'll bet that man we saw was in the car that disappeared!"

Mr. Whipple looked puzzled and the twins' father explained what had happened. Freddie described the scary-looking man with the tie clip shaped like a horse's head.

"With a ruby eye," Bert added.

"I can't think who he could be," the caretaker mused, "but this is no night for anyone to be outside. I'll call to him."

He walked to the door and flung it open. "Hello out there!" he shouted. "Come in out of the storm, whoever you are!"

CHAPTER IV

FLAPJACKS

THE twins waited breathlessly, dreading to see the strange man walk into the room. But no one appeared.

After a few minutes of suspense, Jack Whipple closed the door and came back to the fire. "I guess he's gone now—whoever he was. I'm sorry about that hole in the road, but I consider myself lucky to have met such a nice family."

"We're lucky too, Mr. Whipple," Nan said, leaning over to pat Snap.

"I wish you children would call me Uncle Jack, the way the Meredith children used to," the caretaker said wistfully.

Bert had been examining some odd-looking stone objects on the broad mantel. At Mr. Whipple's words he turned and said, "I think that's a swell idea, Uncle Jack!"

"So do we!" the other three children chorused.

31

Mr. Bobbsey laughed. "That idea met with unanimous approval, Jack."

"Now you have a 'dopted family, Uncle Jack," Flossie announced. "And two sets of twins!"

"That's wonderful!" Mr. Whipple exclaimed heartily.

"Did these come from the West, Uncle Jack? They look like Indian relics," Bert asked, holding up one of the stones.

"Yes, Bert. I found those in Oregon when I was about your age," the caretaker replied. "Those are tools which the early Indians carved out of stone. I'm told there is a large collection of Indian relics in the Museum of Natural History in New York," he continued.

"Maybe we're going to New York soon," Freddie spoke up.

"Well, if you do, be sure to go to that museum," Uncle Jack advised.

"We'll put it at the top of the list," Mr. Bobbsey assured him.

"How did you happen to come East, Mr. Whipple?" Mrs. Bobbsey asked.

Uncle Jack chuckled. "I met Mr. Meredith on a ranch out West and he persuaded me to come back with him and act as caretaker of this estate. I said I'd try it for a year." He scratched his head. "But I got very fond of the Meredith family and I never did go back West."

"Did you hunt for your little brother and sister any more?" Flossie inquired.

The caretaker shook his head. "I'd exhausted every lead by that time. I did hear a rumor that my sister had married and moved to New York City, but no one knew her husband's name. So that clue came to nothing. I even thought her twin might have gone there, too, but I couldn't find him."

Nan had been looking at a photograph which stood on the mantel. She brought it over to Jack Whipple. "Is this a picture of you and the twins?" she asked.

The man took the picture and turned it over. "Yes," he said. "See, our names are written here: Dodie, Davey, and Jack Jim. It was taken when I was twelve and the twins were six."

The other children came running to see the picture. "You all look very nice," Flossie observed as she examined the photograph.

Just then Mr. Bobbsey came back from the telephone. "The garage can't send anyone for some time, Jack. I'm sorry to impose on you this way."

"Think nothing of it!" Mr. Whipple exclaimed. "I'm glad to have your company." He rumpled Freddie's blond hair affectionately.

"Uncle Jack, did the twins call you Jack Jim?" Freddie asked.

"Yes. My full name is John James Whipple.

They nicknamed me Jack Jim. I used to make flapjacks for them when Mother was cooking at the lumber camp. They loved them and when they wanted more they'd shout, "More flap jims, Jack Jim. It was a great joke with them!"

"I like flapjacks too," Freddie said wistfully.

"Well now, that's good! What say we have some right now?" the jolly man proposed.

"Oh, goody!" Flossie jumped up and clapped her hands. "I'll help you!"

Mr. Bobbsey looked at his watch. "It's after five," he said. "I'll call Dinah and see if Mr. Hanks has phoned."

While he put in the call, Mrs. Bobbsey and the twins followed Uncle Jack into his neat little kitchen. Whistling cheerfully, the caretaker put on a white butcher's apron and handed Nan a red and white checked tablecloth.

"Put that on the big table, will you, Nan? And you'll find spoons and forks in the drawer."

Uncle Jack set to work busily sifting flour and beating eggs. Mrs. Bobbsey and the girls quickly set the table. When the batter was mixed, their host put the griddle on the fire. In a few minutes it was piping hot.

"Bring me that bowl of batter, Freddie," Uncle Jack called. "It's time to cook the flapjacks!"

Freddie put both arms around the big bowl

and started across the kitchen. At that moment Mr. Bobbsey came into the room. "Well, children," he called, "we're going to New York!"

"Oh, Daddy, how marvelous!" Flossie cried.

Forgetting that he was holding the bowl, Freddie tried to clap his hands. *Crash!* The bowl fell to the floor and the creamy batter streamed over the linoleum!

"Boy! What a mess!" Bert exclaimed.

"I'm awful sorry, Uncle Jack," Freddie murmured as he tried to hold back the tears.

"It doesn't matter at all," Mr. Whipple consoled him. "We'll clean this up in a jiffy and make some more!"

In the meantime Snap, having heard the clatter, left the fireplace and ran into the kitchen. Eagerly he began to lap up the batter. Bert chased him, and Mr. Whipple found a mop. In a few minutes the floor was spotless again and another bowl of pancake batter was ready.

"Come over here, young fellow," Uncle Jack called to Freddie. "I want you to help me."

With a sweep of the spoon, the cook poured some batter onto the sizzling griddle. "Now watch this!" he said.

As the Bobbseys gathered around, Uncle Jack slipped his spatula under the cake on the griddle and flipped it high into the air. The pancake turned and landed neatly back on the griddle. After a moment he flipped it again and this time it went onto a large blue and white platter which he held in his other hand.

"Now Freddie," he said, "let's see you do that!"

Gingerly Freddie took the spatula while Uncle Jack poured more batter onto the griddle. The little boy slipped the turner under the cake and flipped it. Up it went and over, but landed on the edge of the griddle.

The cook quickly pushed it onto the surface and poured more batter. This time when Freddie flipped it the cake landed precisely in the center of the griddle! Everyone cheered.

In a short while, with both Uncle Jack and Freddie flipping the cakes, there was a large pile of golden brown pancakes. The group gathered around the table and began to eat the delicious flapjacks topped with butter and maple syrup.

Presently Bert said, "Dad, tell us about the New York trip. When will we go?"

"Dinah said Mr. Hanks called and left the message that he would like to see me in New York on Monday morning."

"That means we'll have to take a train tomorrow night, Richard!" Mrs. Bobbsey exclaimed.

"Right!"

"Oh Daddy, how exciting!" cried Nan.

"That's great, Dad!" Bert exclaimed.

The small twins interrupted their eating long enough to clap their hands and grin with delight.

"We'll have to make our reservations as soon as we get back to Lakeport," Mr. Bobbsey decided.

Snap had been sitting quietly on the floor at Jack Whipple's feet. But the smell of the food and the children's cries of excitement were too much for him. He shifted his weight uneasily and gave a low bark.

"Poor Snap!" the caretaker said. "He wants some supper, too. Come over here, boy. I have something for you."

Snap followed the man to the other side of the kitchen where he was given a bowl of chopped meat and cereal.

When the pancakes were finished, the Bobbsey family and Jack Whipple went back into the cozy living room. Snap, having gulped his food hungrily, had stretched out in front of the fire once more.

"That was a fine supper, Jack," Mr. Bobbsey remarked. "You've certainly made our wait very pleasant."

"Look at Snap," Mrs. Bobbsey said suddenly. "He hears something outside."

The dog was growling softly. He had raised his head and was looking intently at the door. All at once he leaped to his feet and ran across the room, growling more fiercely.

"Snap, come here," Mr. Bobbsey said sternly as the dog began to paw wildly at the door.

Uncle Jack went quickly to open it. "Probably the man from the garage," he said as he swung the door wide.

No one was there and Snap rushed out, barking excitedly. The rain had stopped, but the wind was still high—and it was almost as dark as night.

"Snap! Snap! Come back here!" Mr. Bobbsey called from the porch.

Bert whistled for their pet, but Snap did not

return. Then the barking stopped suddenly with a sharp yelp. There was no sound but the wind in the trees.

"Snap's been hurt!" Bert cried, dashing down the steps. "I'm going to find him!"

CHAPTER V

NAN'S CLUE

"HERE Snap! Come Snap!" Bert called, running down the wet path.

As he reached the road the boy heard a low whine. Then he saw Snap. The dog lay in the road. When Bert approached him, his pet tried to get up but could not stand.

"Dad! Snap's hurt! We'll have to carry him!" Bert cried, kneeling beside the animal.

Mr. Bobbsey came quickly to help Bert carry the injured dog to the house. Uncle Jack was watching for them and opened the door at once.

"You dear old Snap!" Nan cried as they all gathered around the dog. "You were defending us from somebody. Oh, I hope you're not hurt badly!"

"Put him on this blanket," Uncle Jack directed, spreading a brown wool square on the floor. "That will be more comfortable for him.

Now I'll look at that right hind leg. I'm used to fixing up animals that get hurt."

Snap rolled his eyes and wagged his tail a little as if to reassure his worried family.

Uncle Jack bent over him. "Quiet, boy, I'll try not to hurt you." The caretaker spoke softly as he took the injured leg in gentle hands. Snap winced and whined but still wagged his tail.

Uncle Jack's skilful fingers moved over Snap's right hind leg. "It's not broken," the man said at last. "But he's had an ugly blow from something heavy. Snap, old fellow, I wish you could talk and tell us how it happened."

"Perhaps the limb of a tree fell and struck him," suggested Mrs. Bobbsey as she stroked the shaggy white fur.

"I think he was chasing a bad man, and the man hit him," declared Flossie indignantly.

"So do I, Flossie," Bert agreed. "And I'll bet I know who it was, too. Snap certainly heard something that made him bark and growl. And that something or someone was pretty close to this house."

"Well, whatever or whoever it was," Uncle Jack said, rising from his knees, "I'm going to fix Snap so that leg won't bother him too much."

He went quickly to a well-stocked cupboard and returned with a roll of bandage, a tube of ointment, and a bottle of antiseptic. Then he proceeded to cleanse and dress the open wound.

Freddie watched the caretaker's skilful fingers, then asked, "Uncle Jack, is there anything that you can't do? You can cook and keep house and be a doctor and—and everything!"

Mr. Whipple laughed as he answered, "When you are as old as I am, you will have learned to do a lot of things, too."

The Bobbseys were so interested in watching the bandaging of their pet that they all jumped at the sound of a loud knock on the door. Snap started up but lay down again and tapped his tail on the floor gently. Nan knew that whoever was at the door was harmless, or Snap would have growled and barked.

Uncle Jack opened the door and a man's voice said, "Good evening. I'm from the Berlin garage."

Mr. Bobbsey went to the door. "Yes, I called you. My car's stuck in a hole on the road out near the bend. I'll be right with you." He came into the room to get his hat. "Come on, Bert, the man may need some help in getting the station wagon back onto the road."

Bert sprang up. Uncle Jack fastened the last end of bandage. Then he said to Mr. Bobbsey, "I'll come too. I want to close that gate." He went out with Bert and Mr. Bobbsey.

Flossie picked up the photograph of the three Whipple children and remarked, "Dodie and Davey were cute little twins. I wonder what they look like now that they are all grown up."

Freddie gazed at the picture over her shoulder and then shut his eyes tight. "I'm trying to think how I would know them," he said. "If I met a very old man on the street in New York who looked like Davey I might say, 'Is your name Mr. Davey Whipple?'"

"Oh, Freddie! Davey wouldn't be as old as Uncle Jack and he isn't old at all," Nan protested. "Anyway you couldn't recognize them from this picture."

There was a sound of footsteps on the porch and Uncle Jack came in. "They didn't need me," he told them. "The truck hauled the car out easily. They are looking to see if the jolt loosened anything. So after I locked the gate, I came back to have a little extra visit with my guests."

"I think Dodie looks more like you than like her twin, Uncle Jack," Nan observed, handing him the photograph. "Wasn't he a blond?"

Uncle Jack nodded and smiled. "You are very keen, Nan, to see that in a picture as poor as this one. Davey had fair hair and blue eyes while Dodie—or Dorothy—and I look like my father's side of the family—dark skin and eyes."

"There's the car," Freddie cried, springing

up and opening the door. "And the rain's stopped."

Mr. Bobbsey and Bert came into the cottage. "All set, I think," Mr. Bobbsey said. Then he held out his hand to Uncle Jack. "We are certainly grateful to you for your royal hospitality. I hope we can do you a good turn some day."

"You must come and have dinner with us after we return from New York, Mr. Whipple," Mrs. Bobbsey added.

The jolly caretaker beamed with pleasure as he shook their hands. Freddie suggested hopefully, "Oh, maybe Uncle Jack will come and make flapjacks at our house!"

"That's a funny way to invite him to have dinner with us," Nan laughed. Uncle Jack laughed, too, and Nan liked the way his face crinkled around his eyes.

"Be sure to see the Museum of Natural History in New York," he said. "I'd like a report on it next time I see you."

"We'll look for your little brother and sister in New York," Flossie promised, "although it may be hard to know them now that they're grown up."

"I'm afraid it would be," Uncle Jack remarked. *"But,* if you should just happen to meet a Mr. Whipple who had a brother Jack—" He laughed and Flossie knew he was teasing her.

"Anyway we'll be on the lookout for Whipples," Nan assured him. "The twins might have gone to New York."

Mr. Bobbsey carried Snap carefully out to the car and Uncle Jack insisted that they take the blanket along for him to lie on. Then the Bobbseys said a final good-by to the kindly caretaker and started for home.

"Mr. Jack Whipple is a real gentleman," Mr. Bobbsey said as they drove along through the wet woods. "I'm glad that Mr. Meredith made it possible for him to stay there in the place that he has cared for all these years."

Dinah and her husband Sam, who drove a truck for Mr. Bobbsey's lumberyard, were watching for the Bobbseys from a front window. "My lands!" Dinah exclaimed. "When Mr. Bobbsey told me on the phone you were 'way off stuck in a hole somewhere, I was worried maybe you couldn't get home tonight."

"Sam, will you take Snap in and make him comfortable?" Mr. Bobbsey asked. "He has hurt his leg, but it is bandaged and he's all right. He'd better not walk on it until tomorrow. I've got to go down to the post office and then to the railroad station to get our tickets and reservations. Bert and Nan, you want to come?"

Freddie and Flossie did not beg to go. Both preferred staying at home to tell Dinah and Sam about their exciting day.

At the post office, while Mr. Bobbsey was

mailing his letter, Nan and Bert strolled over to look at some posters on the wall. They were pictures of criminals wanted by the police.

"Bert! Look!" Nan pointed to one of them and grabbed his arm.

Her twin studied the picture. "That's the same man we saw today in the woods!" he exclaimed excitedly. "I'll tell Dad." He dashed across the floor as Mr. Bobbsey turned away from the mail slot.

"Dad! Come see this picture. It's the fellow we saw in the woods!" Bert spoke in a lower tone because some other people had come in.

"It must be the man, Dad," Nan said. "There couldn't be two faces like that!"

Mr. Bobbsey stared at the picture and read in a low voice, "Pete Rocco, alias Dogface Pete. Five feet ten inches tall, weight about 170 pounds. Left cheek badly scarred. Left eyelid droops. Wanted by police of three states on charges of burglary and mail fraud."

"I'm sure it's the same man," Bert insisted.

"Well, if you're sure, son," his father answered, "you'd better report the incident to the police."

On the way home Mr. Bobbsey stopped at the police station and Nan and Bert went in to tell Police Chief Smith their suspicions.

"Well now," he said, "you're good detectives. We'll start work on this right away and let you know if we catch this man Rocco."

"We're leaving for New York tomorrow," Nan explained, "but we'll call you as soon as we get back."

Nan and Bert almost forgot about the man in the excitement of planning for their trip. The suitcases were brought down, and after church the packing was started.

"I want to take my fire engine," declared

Freddie. "I'd rather take that than a lot of clothes."

"You won't need a fire engine," Bert told him. "The New York Fire Department is one of the finest in the world."

"You will need clothes, Freddie," Nan advised. "You'll have to be more dressed up staying at a hotel than you are at home."

"Oh shucks!" said Freddie, but gave up the idea of taking his fire engine when he heard there would be no time to play with it.

Flossie sighed. "Then I guess I won't take my doll either."

The train for New York did not leave Lakeport until late at night, but the sleeping cars were made up early. The Bobbseys went to the station in time to put Flossie and Freddie to bed at their usual hour. The children had great fun climbing into the berths and looking out the windows.

The car in which the Bobbseys' berths were located was well down the tracks from the station and away from the bright lights. Shortly after the younger twins had fallen asleep, Nan got into her berth. She snapped out the little light and raised the shade to watch the early passengers come down the platform and board the train. It was exciting to see and yet not be seen.

Soon Nan grew sleepy and was about to settle down into her pillow when she heard footsteps outside the window. Once more she raised the shade to look out. A man carrying two very heavy suitcases was coming down the platform toward her. He seemed rather uncertain and stopped once or twice to look over his shoulder.

Nan had an odd feeling that he looked familiar but she could not see his face to find out. The man's hat brim was pulled far down and his coat collar was turned up, although the night was not at all cold.

Suddenly Nan knew where she had seen the man. In the Meredith woods! Was he Dogface Pete and was he going to New York on the same train?

CHAPTER VI

LIBERTY ISLAND

THE NEXT time Nan looked out onto the dimly lighted station platform she saw that the man had stopped. He seemed undecided what to do. He set the heavy bags down, and as he lifted his head Nan caught a glimpse of a rather large mustache. As neither the man in the woods nor Dogface Pete had worn one, she decided that her imagination had played tricks on her. She was about to lie down again when the man picked up the suitcases and suddenly walked away from the train.

"Nan Bobbsey, you stop making up things and go to sleep," she told herself. Then she added, with a yawn, "Just the same, he looked a lot like that awful man with the scarred face."

The next thing Nan knew Mrs. Bobbsey was patting her and saying, "Time to get up, dear. We'll be in New York in an hour."

Nan peered out the curtain to find her mother and Flossie dressed and ready for breakfast. As soon as she was dressed they joined Mr. Bobbsey and the boys in the dining car for a quick breakfast.

The train pulled into the busy Pennsylvania Station right on time and the twins realized that at last they were in the great city. As they left the escalators and walked through the huge station Nan and Flossie caught sight of a shop window filled with miniature animals.

"Oh!" Flossie squealed. "See the darling little horses and cows, Nan!"

Her sister ran with her to look in the window. "Mother," she said, "may Flossie and I get some for our collection?" The two Bobbsey girls took great pride in the decoration of the bedroom they shared at home. They had been collecting miniature toys for their shelves for some time.

Mrs. Bobbsey smiled and turned to her husband. "I'll stop here with the girls. We'll meet you and the boys under the big clock in a few minutes."

"We'll have to wait for the porter with our luggage anyway," Mr. Bobbsey replied. "Go ahead." He went with Freddie and Bert to be away from the stream of people.

"Everybody in New York's in a hurry!" Freddie remarked.

One quick-moving man in particular attracted the boys' attention. His hat brim was turned far down and his coat collar was up around his chin. He carried two heavy suitcases. As he passed them, the stranger looked up and Bert saw with a start that the man's left eyelid drooped. Bert saw, too, that the stranger had a brown mustache which covered his mouth. The lower part of his face was partly hidden by his turned-up coat collar.

The man had scarcely gone by them when Freddie pulled Bert's arm and said in a hoarse whisper, "Did you see that tie clasp he was wearing, Bert? It was exactly like the one the man in the woods had on! I saw it through the opening in his coat."

"It's the same man!" Bert exclaimed. "I'm going to follow him."

At this moment Mrs. Bobbsey and the two girls joined them. Bert grabbed Nan's arm. "Hurry! Follow me!" he said. "See that man with two suitcases ahead there? It's Dogface Pete or I'm a blue jay! He's going up the stairs."

The twins walked very fast, and Freddie ran to keep up with them. Mr. and Mrs. Bobbsey and Flossie followed, wondering what had happened.

"That's the same man I saw on the station platform at Lakeport last night," Nan told her twin breathlessly as they ran up the stairs to the upper level. When they reached the top step they saw the man going out the door toward the taxi stand. They hurried after him.

As the other Bobbseys went up the stairs, Mrs. Bobbsey said to her husband, "Why are Nan and the boys rushing so? I'm afraid we'll lose them."

Mr. Bobbsey shrugged. "Maybe they saw the porter with our luggage."

The three young detectives arrived at the curb just in time to see the man they were following jump into a taxi and slam the door. He sank back into a corner of the car as it passed the children.

"He's gone," Bert announced to his father as the three other Bobbseys came out to join them, and explained about Dogface.

"What were you planning to do if you did catch him?" his father asked.

"I wanted to find out where he was going. I thought maybe we could hear the address he gave the driver," Bert explained.

"I'll report this to the police," Mr. Bobbsey said and disappeared into the station.

As he was returning, the red cap came with their luggage and Mr. Bobbsey hailed a cab. After they had all piled in and were on their way to a hotel, the conversation turned again to the strange man.

"It's odd," Bert mused. "I didn't see any purple mark on this man's face and Dogface's picture had none."

"Maybe the mark we saw on the man's face in the Meredith woods wasn't a permanent one," Nan suggested. "Perhaps he had been eating something like blackberries when we saw him."

"Oh," squealed Flossie, "maybe he was the one who stole our blueberry pie!"

"Wow!" Bert exclaimed. "I think that's right, Flossie. I'll bet he went past the picnic grounds on his way to the Meredith place and saw the pie there on the table. Of course he took it!"

Mrs. Bobbsey laughed. "Well, the Bobbsey Detective Agency seems to have solved the blueberry pie mystery anyway!"

They all had to laugh at this. Then Mr. Bobbsey said, "Now that I've told the police about the man in the Meredith woods, I suggest we forget him. We're here to enjoy New York. And if you must solve a mystery, keep your ears open for the name Whipple."

"Oh that's right," said Nan. "Wouldn't it be wonderful to find Uncle Jack's brother and sister?"

The twins looked out the windows, fascinated by the buildings that reached into the sky.

"I think you should see what everyone coming

to New York by boat sees first," Mr. Bobbsey said. "Perhaps your mother will take you on the ferry to Liberty Island to see the Statue of Liberty today. I have an appointment in lower Manhattan and can take you to the wharf at the Battery."

"That will be neat," said Bert.

The taxi pulled up in front of a large hotel, and in a short time the Bobbseys were in their rooms which overlooked Central Park. Running to the window, Flossie exclaimed, "Oh see the park with all the high buildings around it!"

"And a lake in it," Freddie added. "Let's play there some time."

The unpacking was quickly done and the Bobbseys went out to take a subway. The idea of being way down under the ground and going so fast below the city traffic intrigued the twins.

As they came up onto the street again to go to the wharf, Freddie asked, "Dad, how do they fix it so people get fresh air under the ground?"

"See that tower over there?" Mr. Bobbsey pointed to a large concrete object not far away. "Inside it are machines which send air down into the subways."

"There's the Statue of Liberty!" Bert exclaimed. "She doesn't look very big from here."

Across the bay the figure of Miss Liberty holding her torch aloft, stood out against the blue of the sky. As the Bobbseys gazed at it a small steamer cut through the waters of the bay toward them.

"That's the ferry," Mr. Bobbsey said. "I'll get your tickets." He left them for a few moments to go to a nearby ticket window. When he returned he remarked, "I'm sorry I can't go with you. But I'll meet you here around noon. There's a good restaurant nearby where we can have lunch out of doors."

New York Bay was a busy place, as the twins discovered while riding across the water. Great

ships made their way toward the open ocean. Important-looking tugs bustled about, blowing whistles while they pulled or pushed flat barge-like boats loaded with cargo.

Above them all the towering Statue of Liberty gazed down serenely. "She looks green," said Bert. "I thought the statue was made of copper."

"She is," his mother replied. "But you remember from your school work that copper oxidizes in the moist air and turns to that soft green color."

"Oh!" Nan exclaimed. "Look at New York from here!"

The tall, narrow buildings of lower Manhattan rose into the blue sky like giant fingers. "The skyline *is* beautiful!" Mrs. Bobbsey agreed.

"It doesn't look real," Flossie remarked. "More like great, great big toys."

As the ferry drew up to the dock on Liberty Island, the statue loomed impressively above the sightseers.

"We can go up inside," Bert said. "I'd like to climb to the tip of the torch."

"So would I," Freddie stated. "And I'm going to."

They went ashore and walked with the crowd into the base of the statue. There an elevator took them up ten stories to the top of the pedestal.

After a brief look at New York and the bay from the balcony, the Bobbseys started the long climb up the spiral stairway to the goddess's crown.

To Bert's and Freddie's great disappointment the entrance to the right arm, which held the torch, was blocked by a heavy gate and a *No Admittance* sign.

"It's been closed to visitors for years," one of the guards told the two boys.

"Oh well," Bert remarked, "we'll go up to the tip of her crown anyway."

Freddie did not say anything, but paused a moment to look at the gate which blocked the way. He wondered if he might be able to squirm under it!

"Come!" called Mrs. Bobbsey and she and the twins went on up, up, up the narrow winding stairs in the dark tunnellike interior.

When they finally arrived at the room inside the crest of the statue's head it was already filled with people. The Bobbseys waited their turn, then went to the side to look out the windows.

Far, far below them lay the blue bay with boats that looked very tiny. In the Narrows, the waterway to the ocean, two steamships were passing. Their whistled salutes were as faint as the boats were small.

"I'd like to drop a stone down from here and see how long it would take to reach the water, wouldn't you, Freddie?" Bert turned to his brother, who he thought was beside him. A strange little boy looked up at him. Freddie was nowhere in sight!

After one look from the window of the diadem Freddie had gone back down the winding stairway to the entrance to the right arm. A guard was there unlocking the gate to allow three men with photographic equipment to enter. Without a word Freddie followed the men to the staircase and began to mount it behind them. The guard had not turned around after the men entered so did not see the little boy.

There were no curves in these stairs. Freddie's legs began to get very tired but he went on up steadily. As the men stepped out onto a tiny balcony, he slipped out, too, and around to the opposite side. He did not want the photographers to see him.

"What a view!" one of them exclaimed. "It's like being in an airplane."

Freddie peeked around from the back of the torch and caught his breath at the sight of New York so far below. He could look down on the goddess's diadem where he had left his family looking through the windows. He wished that they could come up to see the view from this balcony.

Freddie's legs were so tired they ached so he

sat down in the sunshine to rest. Way in the distance he could see the blue ocean beyond the land. It looked so calm and peaceful that it made him sleepy. His eyes closed and he slid down in a heap, curled up like a puppy.

The photographers finished their pictures and climbed down to the iron gate. The guard, who had been waiting for them, unlocked it to let them out. Then he relocked it and went down to other duties. High above, Freddie was alone —and sound asleep.

CHAPTER VII

FIRE!

WHEN Bert could not find his brother, he hurried over to Nan. "Where's Freddie?" he asked.

She turned from the window in surprise. "I thought he was next to you, Bert," she answered.

"Is Freddie lost?" Flossie cried anxiously.

Mrs. Bobbsey took the little girl's hand and said reassuringly, "Freddie must have gone downstairs to the other balcony. He's probably waiting for us there."

The group went down the steps to the top of the pedestal and out onto the little gallery which ran around it. Freddie was not there. They descended to the promenade which circled the statue at the base of the pedestal. Bert went one way and Nan the other, past the benches. They were filled with people, but Freddie was not among them.

"What's the matter, buddy? Did you lose

someone?" a guard asked Bert, seeing his worried expression.

Bert nodded. "My brother. He's about six years old, light hair and blue eyes. He was wearing a red and white striped sweater."

"Oh, he's somewhere around. Kids get lost here every day. Did you look on the benches?" asked the guard walking along beside him. "Your brother might be asleep on one of them."

"We've looked there," Bert said. "Say, is there any way that he could have gone up to the torch?"

"No," the guard replied. "No one's admitted up there."

"If he could find a way, Freddie wouldn't stop for that reason," Bert told the man. "Could he possibly crawl under the gate?"

"I don't see how. I was around that gate for a couple of hours this morning," the guard said. "Some photographers went up to the torch to take pictures and I had to wait to unlock the gate when they came down."

"You're sure there wasn't a little boy with them?" Mrs. Bobbsey asked, now thoroughly alarmed.

"How could he have gone past without my seeing him?" the guard said. "But I'll take a look if you're sure you've hunted everywhere else for him."

"May I go too?" Bert wanted to know as they walked rapidly toward the entrance to the torch.

"If there aren't any people around, you can," the guard told him. They went up the stairs to the top of the pedestal. The crowd was thinning out, because it was nearly noon. When they reached the barred entrance to the arm, there was no one else in sight.

"Come on," said the guard and led the way up the stairs. When they stepped out onto the small balcony he looked about. "No one here, sonny," he observed.

Bert wasted no time looking at New York from this pinnacle but went round to the other side of the balcony. There was Freddie, sound asleep!

"Well I'll be blowed!" shouted the guard in amazement.

Freddie opened his eyes and saw Bert standing there. "Hello, Bert," he piped. "How did you get here? You're not allowed."

The guard burst into a loud guffaw. "I'll say you aren't," he roared. "How *did* you get up here, young fellow?"

Freddie's face turned red but he answered bravely, "I came up with those men who took pictures. Where are they?"

"They've been gone for some time," the guard informed him. "You might have been shut up here until the next time the lights had to be changed in the torch!"

"Oh, would you and Mother have gone back without me, Bert?" Freddie's round little face looked frightened.

"No, of course not," Bert assured his brother. "But you shouldn't have left without telling us where you were going."

"I'm sorry," Freddie said, hanging his head.

The guard led the way down the stairs. At the bottom Bert and Freddie thanked him, and then ran to where Mrs. Bobbsey and the girls were waiting on the promenade.

Freddie's mother listened to his story with a

serious expression on her face. Then she said, "Freddie, I want you to promise me that you won't do such a thing again. You must stay with the family all the time we are in New York."

"Yes, Mother, I promise," Freddie agreed. "I'm sorry you were worried."

Mr. Bobbsey was waiting at the New York City dock when the ferry reached Manhattan. He led his family to the outdoor restaurant where they sat down at a table under a striped umbrella.

"Well, how was Miss Liberty?" he asked when they had given the waitress their order.

"Just wonderful!" Nan exclaimed. "Did you know that she is one hundred and fifty-two feet tall?"

"And her face is ten feet wide!" Bert added.

"She's really a big lady!" Mr. Bobbsey laughed.

When they had finished their luncheon of sandwiches and milk, Mr. Bobbsey suggested a walk around lower Manhattan. "You know this section was first settled when the Dutch founded the town of New Amsterdam here," he explained.

"What is that tiny park all fenced in?" Nan asked. "Can't anyone go inside?"

"That's Bowling Green, a very historic patch of grass," her father told them. "It was used as a bowling green in the early days. The old fort stood beside it. When the British occupied New York they put a statue of the king there with a fence around it."

"Do you suppose this is the same fence?" Nan mused.

"Oh no. During the American Revolution the people of New York pulled down the statue, fence and all," Mr. Bobbsey replied. "They didn't like His Majesty, George the Third."

"History is sure more interesting when you see the places where things happened!" Bert observed.

The Bobbseys took the subway back to their hotel. Later, when Nan and Flossie were ready for dinner, Nan took the big telephone directory from the small table in the room and sat down.

"I'm going to look up the Whipples," she explained. "Will you see if Bert can come in, Flossie?"

Flossie ran out and soon returned with Nan's twin. When Nan explained what she was doing Bert offered to make the calls.

"Here's a Mr. D. S. Whipple," Nan said. "Maybe his name is David. Let's try him."

Bert put in the call and presently a man answered. "Hello," Bert said. "Is this Mr. D. S. Whipple? Is your name David and if so, do you have a brother Jack?"

"What is this?" the voice at the other end of the line sputtered. "Who told you to call me? I don't have any brothers!"

Bert jumped as the receiver was slammed down in his ear. "Wow!" he said as he put down the telephone. "I'm sure Uncle Jack's brother wouldn't be that kind of a man!"

Flossie giggled. "You looked so funny, Bert, when that man hung up on you!"

Bert grinned. "Are there any more D. Whipples?" he asked Nan who had been scanning the pages of the big book.

"Here's a Henry D. Maybe his middle name is David."

Again Bert asked the operator for the number. He spoke into the mouthpiece. "Is this Mr. Henry D. Whipple? I'm sorry to bother you, but is your middle name David?"

"Sorry son," a polite voice answered. "My name is Henry Dennis. Is this a guessing game?"

"Oh no, sir," Bert replied hastily. "I am trying to locate someone. I have the wrong number."

"Here's another," Nan said as Bert replaced the receiver. "Albert D. Whipple. Try him."

Bert called the number. In reply to his question a pleasant voice answered, "Well now, that's an idea! I don't really have a middle name—

just use an initial to make it sound better! Perhaps it should be David!"

Bert laughed. "Thank you, sir. I guess you're not the man I'm trying to find. I hope I didn't disturb you."

"Think nothing of it!" the man said breezily and hung up.

"We don't seem to be having much luck," Bert observed as he turned away from the phone. "Probably Uncle Jack's brother isn't in New York!"

The next morning Mr. Bobbsey announced that he had another business engagement. Since it was raining he suggested that Mrs. Bobbsey take the twins to Radio City Music Hall. "There's a good movie, and the stage show is always interesting," he said.

The children were delighted at this way of spending a rainy day in the big city. "There's sure a lot to see and do here," Bert remarked. "How do the kids that live in New York ever have time to get any school work done?"

Mrs. Bobbsey smiled. "I'm sure they don't go sightseeing enough to interfere with their home work."

The feature picture at the Music Hall was an exciting Western and the twins sat spellbound watching it. Several people came into the darkened theater, and two—an elderly woman and a little boy—sat at the end of the Bobbseys' row.

When the lights came on at the end of the picture Freddie looked at the boy about his own age sitting next to him. "Oh, I know you!" he said. "I saw you yesterday in the elevator at our hotel."

The boy smiled. "I saw you too," he said shyly. Then turning to the woman on his other side, he explained, "Grandma, this is the boy I told you I saw in the elevator."

The woman leaned forward and smiled. "My grandson is Bruce Dickerson," she said. "What is your name?"

"I'm Freddie Bobbsey. And this is my mother and my twin sister, Flossie. Farther down are Nan and Bert. They're twins too." Freddie was quite breathless after this long introduction.

Bruce's grandmother and Mrs. Bobbsey laughed and nodded to each other. The older woman leaned over to say, "You have a wonderful family, Mrs. Bobbsey! I wish that you'd let Freddie and Flossie come to lunch with Bruce today. He is visiting me in my apartment at the hotel, and I'm afraid he gets very lonely. The children can play together this afternoon. Then if it clears, my maid Elsie can take them to Central Park."

"That would be delightful," Mrs. Bobbsey said, and Freddie squealed with excitement.

The stage show began. There was a funny man doing imitations of animals. This made Freddie and Bruce laugh so hard that the people in front of them turned around to smile at the two little boys.

The weather had begun to clear by the time the group left the theatre. On their arrival at the hotel, Freddie and Flossie hurried to their rooms to get ready for luncheon and were soon enjoying a big meal with Bruce in his grandmother's apartment.

When they had finished eating, the children went into Bruce's room to play. "Goodness!" Freddie exclaimed. "What a lot of toys you have! Did you bring them all with you?"

Bruce laughed. "I didn't have to bring any. My grandfather has a big store here in New York where they have lots of toys. He gives them to me."

"My favorite toy is my fire engine," Freddie told him. "I can put out real fires with it, can't I, Flossie?"

His twin nodded. "Oh yes. Daddy calls Freddie his little fireman."

Just then they heard the screech of sirens below. The children ran to the window and saw fire engines racing down the street.

"We can't see anything from here," Bruce complained. "Let's go downstairs."

"Shouldn't we ask your grandmother?" Flossie said doubtfully.

"She's taking a nap," Bruce replied. "I'll tell Elsie we're going."

The children went into the kitchen but Elsie was talking on the telephone. "She doesn't like it if I talk to her when she's on the phone," Bruce whispered. "Come on! She'll see us go."

The three walked past the giggling Elsie who scarcely looked at them, and went out to the elevator. No one paid any attention as the three children crossed the lobby and hurried out into the street.

It had stopped raining and the sun was shining. Crowds of people were hustling toward the end of the block where the fire engines had stopped before a tall building.

"I wish I had my fire engine here," Freddie cried. "I knew I'd need it!"

The crowd grew thicker. Suddenly Flossie was pushed right into the street. A big fireman in a white rubber coat picked her up and set her back on the sidewalk. "Where's your mother, little girl?" he asked. "You'd better run back to her before you get hurt."

Freddie ran up to Flossie and took her hand. "We'll go back to the hotel. Mother wouldn't like us to be here alone."

Bruce caught up to them and took Flossie's

other hand. "We won't let you get hurt. Come on! I'll take you to my grandfather's store. I want to get a fire engine like Freddie's and help fight the fire!"

CHAPTER VIII

THE SIDEWALK ARTIST

FLOSSIE looked doubtful when Bruce announced that he was going to his grandfather's store. "Do you know the way?" she asked.

"Oh sure. It's down here," Bruce said, leading the twins away from the crowd and around a corner.

Flossie wanted to look at all the wonderful things in the shop windows, but Bruce hurried her along.

They were very careful to cross the streets with the green lights, but suddenly a big, burly policeman took hold of Bruce's arm. "Where are you kids going?" he asked.

"To my grandfather's store," the little boy replied. "I go there lots of times."

"Better wait for your mother. Where is she?" Still holding Bruce's arm, the officer looked around.

"I can't wait for her. She's way off on the Pacific Ocean." The boy slipped from the policeman's grasp and the three went on their way.

"Watch the lights now," the officer called after them.

"Yes sir," Freddie replied. "We always do."

It seemed to him and his twin that they had walked far enough to reach Lakeport by the time Bruce finally announced, "Here it is." He led them into a large store thronged with customers.

"Granddad's office is on the eleventh floor," Bruce said importantly. "We'll have to take the elevator."

The twins followed their friend to the back of the store but there were no elevators. "Oh, I guess they're on the side," Bruce remarked.

In a few minutes they found the elevators and rode one of the cars to the eleventh floor. When the children stepped out, Bruce looked around. "Is my Grandfather Dickerson here?" he asked a young woman sitting at a desk nearby.

She smiled and asked, "Whom do you want to see, sonny?"

"I want my Grandfather Dickerson," Bruce repeated. "His office is on the eleventh floor."

Just then two men came up to the desk. "Do you know anyone named Dickerson who has an office on this floor?" the girl asked them.

They both shook their heads. "You children must be lost. Are you sure you're in the right place?"

"Yes!" Bruce protested. "I want my grand-dad." The little boy burst into tears.

Just then the elevator doors opened and two men stepped out. "Well, well, what's all this about?" asked one of them gently. "Who are these young visitors?"

Freddie looked up into his kind face. "I'm Freddie Bobbsey and this is my twin sister, Flossie. We came with Bruce to his grandfather's store but now he can't find his grandfather."

"What is Bruce's grandfather's name?" asked the gentleman.

Bruce was still crying, so Freddie answered. "He is Granddad Dickerson."

"Oh, Bruce Dickerson!" exclaimed the kind man. "I know him well. You're in the wrong store, children. Mr. Dickerson's store is about three blocks from here. Does anyone know you're here?"

"N-no," Freddie answered.

The man opened the door to a nearby office. "Come in here, all of you, while I telephone Bruce's grandmother," he said. "She didn't know that you were coming, did she?"

"N-no," Bruce managed to reply. "She was taking a nap. We went down to see a fire and then I wanted a fire engine like Freddie's, so we came to get one from my granddad's store."

"I see," the man said smiling. "I'll call Mrs. Dickerson and explain where you are. Then we'll look down in our toy department. Maybe we have fire engines, too."

Bruce's eyes sparkled through his tears. The three children sat very still until the telephone conversation was finished. Then the man came over to where they sat. "My name is John Wagner, children. I have just told your grandmother, Bruce, that I would take you back to the hotel. But first we have some shopping to do. Come along."

He led them into the elevator and down to the basement where toys were sold. "Oh!" Flossie exclaimed. She had never seen so many playthings all at once in her life.

"Which one do you want, Bruce?" Mr. Wagner asked as they paused in front of a display of fire engines of all sizes.

Freddie saw one like his. He did not say anything but was glad when Bruce chose that one.

"That's 'zactly like Freddie's," Flossie said.

"Now, Flossie, how about a doll for you?" asked Mr. Wagner. He took a beautiful little girl doll from a counter.

"Oh, oh!" Flossie hugged it to her. "I didn't 'spect to get anything, Mr. John," she said.

"You deserve it after that long walk," he said. "Now how about you, Freddie?"

Freddie answered shyly, "I'd like a small police whistle, if you please, Mr. Wagner."

"Righto! I'm sure we must have them," John Wagner said and led the children straight to the right counter. "Here you are."

Freddie's eyes sparkled at the new toy.

"Don't blow it in here," said Mr. Wagner teasingly. "You don't want the police to know you ran away!"

Meanwhile, the other Bobbseys had not heard of Freddie's and Flossie's adventure. Soon after the small twins had gone to Bruce's apartment for luncheon, Mrs. Bobbsey had turned to the older twins and asked, "How would you two like to go down to Greenwich Village?"

"Where's that?" Bert wanted to know.

"It's in lower Manhattan, not too far from where we were yesterday, but it's the section of New York where many artists live," his mother explained.

"Oh let's!" Nan exclaimed. "I'd love that!"

Bert agreed, so after lunch the three walked to Fifth Avenue and took a bus down to Washington Square.

"Oh look!" Nan cried. "They're having an exhibition of paintings!"

Propped up against the buildings around the

square were pictures of all kinds. Some of the artists stood near their works of art. Many of the men wore full beards. The women were in bright, colored smocks.

The twins and their mother walked along slowly, admiring the paintings on display. "Would you each like to buy one as a memento of your visit to New York?" Mrs. Bobbsey asked.

"How nice, Mother!" Nan exclaimed. "I know exactly the one I want. I saw it back there a minute ago."

They all turned and retraced their steps until she found the picture. It was the head and shoulders of a man with gray hair and smiling brown eyes. Behind him was the brown shingled wall of a cottage.

"I think he looks just like Uncle Jack," Nan explained. "May I get it?"

Mrs. Bobbsey studied the sketch. "It is very well done and looks amazingly like Mr. Whipple. If it's your choice, you may buy it." She gave the money to Nan who went to pay the dark, slender young artist who stood nearby.

"I'm so glad you like it," the blue-smocked young woman said. "I painted it last summer when I was visiting friends at Lake Metoka. The man is caretaker of a nearby estate."

"Then it *is* Uncle Jack!" Nan exclaimed.

"That makes it even nicer, doesn't it, Mom?"

The artist smiled again. "Oh, do you know him? How interesting! His name is Jack Whipple. He let me make the sketch when I told him I was going to illustrate a book and needed a picture of an older man."

"We'll tell him we have his picture when we see him again," Mrs. Bobbsey said. "Now, Bert, it's your turn to select one."

They wandered on until Bert saw a picture he liked. It was a small oil painting of the East River with its busy tugs and graceful bridges.

"I often paint the East River," the young bearded artist told them as he wrapped the picture. "I think it's one of the most interesting parts of New York."

Nearby stood a fat, jolly-looking man in a beret and a faded artist's smock. "How would you children like your portrait painted?" he called. "I'll do the two of you for the price of one since you're twins!"

Mrs. Bobbsey laughed. "That's what I'd like for my souvenir," she said. "Go on over there and pose, Bert and Nan."

Smilingly the twins complied, and in five minutes the artist whipped the sketch off his easel and handed it to Mrs. Bobbsey with a flourish. "Why, it's wonderful!" she exclaimed in delight. "I'll always treasure this."

Later as they walked from the bus to their hotel carrying the prized purchases, Bert remarked, "Look who's getting out of that taxi in front! It's Freddie and Flossie with Bruce and a strange man."

"And there's Mrs. Dickerson coming out to meet them," Nan said in surprise.

When Mrs. Bobbsey and the older twins reached the hotel, Mrs. Dickerson introduced the man as Mr. John Wagner. "I'm afraid you won't allow your children to play with my grandson again," she said apologetically.

Mr. Wagner spoke up quickly. "Please don't be so hard on Bruce, Mrs. Dickerson. I've had

a very happy afternoon with him and the Bobbsey twins."

Mrs. Bobbsey looked so bewildered that Mrs.
Dickerson laughed and said, "I'll tell you all
about it after we go inside."

Nan and Bert strolled into the lobby, while
Bruce and the younger twins waited to say
good-by to Mr. Wagner. A man was registering
at the desk. As they passed him, Nan heard the
man say something about wiring from California for a room.

The clerk replied, "Yes, Mr. Whipple. We
have room 1022 for you."

Nan grabbed Bert's arm. "Did you hear?" she
whispered. "He called that man Mr. Whipple!"

At that moment, Freddie and Flossie came
running in with Bruce. Mrs. Dickerson and Mrs.
Bobbsey, talking earnestly, were close behind
them.

"See my new dolly, Nan," Flossie cried, holding it up for her sister to look at. "Mr. John
bought it at the store that wasn't Bruce's grandfather's. I'm going to call her Joan because that's
girl for John."

"Wow! Where did you get all the toys?" Bert
asked when he spied the fire engine and the
shiny police whistle.

Mrs. Bobbsey spoke up quickly. "They'll tell
you all about it when we get upstairs, Bert. Are

you and Nan coming up to the room with us?"

"We'll be up in just a minute," Bert assured her.

"Well, don't be long. It's almost time to get ready for dinner," she said, leading the younger twins toward the elevator.

"Bert!" Nan said in a low voice. "You must ask that man if he has a brother Jack. He's finished registering now."

"All right—if you're sure," her twin replied. He walked over to the tall, ruddy-faced man who was just putting a wallet back into his pocket.

"Excuse me, sir," Bert said politely. "I overheard the room clerk call you Mr. Whipple. Do you have a brother named Jack?"

CHAPTER IX

THE GOAT WAGON

HEARING Bert's question, the man looked up in surprise. When he saw the boy's embarrassed expression he smiled.

"I'm afraid you heard wrong," he said. "My name is Whittle, not Whipple. And I don't have a brother Jack. But I have a son by that name." He motioned to a tall boy of about fifteen standing nearby.

"Come here, Jack. I want you to meet—"

"I'm Bert Bobbsey and this is my sister Nan," Bert said. "I'm sorry to have bothered you, sir," he added regretfully.

"Well now, you haven't bothered me at all," Mr. Whittle replied kindly. "I'm sorry I'm not the man you want."

"We're looking for a Mr. David Whipple," Nan volunteered. "We promised his brother Jack we'd try to find him."

"Have you looked in all the New York area

telephone directories?" Jack Whittle suggested.

"We looked in the Manhattan directory," Bert replied, "but we didn't think of the other ones."

"Let's go look now and see what we can find," Jack said. "Maybe I can help you. I often come to New York with my dad."

"In that case, I'll go on to our room, Jack," Mr. Whittle said. "Come up when you've finished."

"Okay, Dad," the boy replied as the three new friends went off to the telephone room. Each took a directory and soon they were poring over the contents.

"Here's a David Whipple on Staten Island," Bert called out. "Where's that?"

"There's none here," Jack said, closing his book. "Staten Island is across the bay. It's a keen ride on a warm day. If you go there, I'd like to go along—if you wouldn't mind."

"That would be fun," Bert agreed enthusiastically. "Let's call on the man."

"How did your friend happen to lose track of this brother?" Jack asked as they sat down on a couch in the lobby of the hotel. "Was it here in New York recently?"

"No, it was way out West," Bert told him. "It happened a long time ago."

Jack looked puzzled. "Why are you hunting for him in New York then?" he asked. "And so long after he disappeared?" He seemed disappointed.

"Maybe it does seem like a wild goose chase to you," Bert said slowly, "but it doesn't to us. We just heard about it last week and we like solving mysteries. Mr. Jack Whipple is a swell man and he's awfully lonely without any family. His married sister Dodie is supposed to be here and Uncle Jack thought his brother Davey might be, too. So we thought we'd look for the Whipple twins."

"They're twins?" asked Jack in surprise. "And both were lost?"

"It's a keen story," Bert told their new friend, "I'll tell you all about it as Uncle Jack told it to us."

Jack Whittle listened carefully as the twins related Uncle Jack's story of his childhood tragedy. When they had finished he said, "I think you're wonderful to spend your time in New York trying to trace these two people. That's some story! When I go back to California I'm going to look up all the Whipples there. People do go there, too, you know," he added jokingly.

The three went up in the elevator together, and Jack left the others at the tenth floor. Before he went Jack said, "It's great meeting you kids here. Dad's always so busy in New York I shift for myself most of the time."

In the Bobbseys' suite Nan and Bert found the younger twins telling Mr. and Mrs. Bobbsey about their exciting day with Bruce. They listened, too.

"Jumping giraffes!" Bert exclaimed.

Then he and Nan told about their meeting with Jack Whittle. "I think he's lonely here by himself," Nan added. "Let's take him around with us sometimes."

"Good idea," her mother answered.

That evening as the Bobbseys went into the dining room, Bert crossed the room to speak to Jack and his father at another table. "We're going to the Museum of Natural History tomorrow, Jack. Would you like to come with us?"

Jack's face lighted up with pleasure. "I sure would."

"Half past nine in the lobby, then," Bert told him. "I'm awfully glad you can go."

Jack was waiting for them the next morning when the Bobbseys came down. The children walked together to the subway station laughing and joking.

As the Bobbsey party stood on the station platform, a gang of rowdy boys going to a baseball game crowded in between the younger twins and the others.

The boys were shouting and pushing so that neither Freddie nor Flossie heard Mr. Bobbsey say, "We take a local to Eighty-first Street. This train coming is an express, so stand back."

The train roared to a stop and the doors opened. Flossie and Freddie were swept into one of the cars by the jostling crowd. Just as the doors slammed shut Mr. Bobbsey saw what had happened, but it was too late. The train moved away with Flossie and Freddie aboard!

They had scrambled to get a seat before the train started, thinking that the rest of the family was right behind them. When they did not see any of them in the crowd Freddie said, "They must be in the next car. We'd better go in there."

The twins made their way to the end door. It was hard to keep their balance for the train was going very fast and swaying from side to side. Freddie tried to open the big door but he could not budge it.

"Where do you think you're going, son?" asked a man sitting close to the door.

"We have to find our family," Freddie replied. "I think they're in the next car."

"What's your name?" the man asked, rising. "You sit here. I'll see if they're in the next car."

"Please ask if Mr. Bobbsey is there," directed Freddie, as he and Flossie climbed onto the seat. The man went out the door and the twins waited anxiously.

After a few moments he returned. "They're

not on this train. I spoke to the motorman about it, and he is going to put you off at the 125th Street station. The agent there will keep you until your folks come. It's the next stop."

"Oh, dear!" Flossie exclaimed, but Freddie said calmly, "Oh, Daddy will find us. He always does."

Before long the motorman blew a loud blast on the train whistle. When the cars came to a stop, a man in uniform was waiting on the platform for Flossie and Freddie.

"Stay here," he told them. "Your father's coming to get you. The man at the 59th Street change booth just phoned."

The twins sat down to wait. Although the train had started as a subway it had come out of the tunnel and now the tracks were high above the street.

"I hear children," said Flossie. "Let's go partway down the stairs and look at them." She went toward the stairs. Freddie followed.

On the street below them was a crowd of shout-

ing youngsters. They were swarming around a
boy of about ten, who was holding a goat by a
halter. A small and rickety cart was hitched behind the animal, which tossed its bearded head
impatiently.

The boy caught sight of the twins on the steps
of the station. "Hi, you!" he called shrilly. "Do
you want a ride with my goat?"

The twins went cautiously down to the bottom
of the stairs. "We can't go away," Freddie told
the boy. "Our father is coming here to get us."

"I won't take you far and it will only be a minute or two," urged the boy with the goat.

"It would be fun," murmured Flossie. "Let's
go, Freddie!"

"Well—" said her twin, but Flossie was on her
way toward the goat cart. The boy helped her
in and almost at once started off, holding the
goat's rope bridle.

Up the street he ran, paying no attention to
red lights or oncoming traffic. Freddie followed.

Flossie was thoroughly frightened. "Stop!"
she cried, pulling at the goat's thin rope reins.

"Wait! Stop!" yelled Freddie pounding along
behind.

The boy and the goat went so fast they seemed
to have wings on their feet. The little cart
jumped and bounced along over the rough pave-
ment.

Finally the boy halted, panting. He seemed surprised to see that Flossie was crying. "Get out," he ordered. Flossie didn't need to be told. She was climbing down as soon as the cart stopped.

As Freddie rushed up the boy said, "All right, now. Fork over the dough."

Flossie and Freddie stared at him. He snapped his fingers. "Give me the money, bud." He held out a very dirty hand expectantly. "It's fifty cents for the ride."

"I haven't got fifty cents," Freddie told him. "We didn't ask to ride on your old goat cart." Freddie put his hand in his pocket and took out ten cents. "This is all I have," he said.

The boy turned to Flossie. "You got any money, sister?" he asked her.

"No," cried Flossie through her tears. "And if I had I wouldn't give it to you. That was a terrible ride!"

"Oho, so you don't like my goat cart!" the boy jeered. With that he grabbed the dime from Freddie's hand and ran off, calling back, "You can find your own way back!"

"I'm glad he's gone," Freddie declared.

"So am I," his twin agreed. "Do you know the way back to the subway station, Freddie?"

"We turned a lot of corners," he answered, "but I guess I can find it."

They started off in the direction from which they had come. "Where can that old station be?" Flossie asked anxiously when they had covered several blocks. "Let's cross this street and go down that way."

There was no traffic light at the corner. The twins waited until they thought it was safe, then started across the street. Suddenly a huge truck came roaring around the corner. Freddie pulled his twin out of its path just in time.

At that moment they heard a familiar sound. Down the street came the shouting crowd of youngsters following the boy and the goat cart. A big policeman had the goat's rope in one hand and with the other he held the boy's arm.

"Ask the policeman the way to the station," Flossie urged.

Freddie ran toward the officer, calling, "Where is the station, Mr. Policeman?"

The officer could not hear him over the yelling of the other children. But a man passing by said, "You want the police station, sonny? Just follow that cop. He's taking the kids there."

Freddie shook his head. "No, I mean the station where the trains are."

"There's no other station around here," the man replied. "Just the police station."

CHAPTER X

LOST AND FOUND

WHEN Flossie heard the man say he did not know where the subway station was, she began to cry. "I guess we're lost, Freddie," she sobbed.

Her twin was discouraged too, but he answered, "It's the station that's lost, Flossie. We'll have to find it."

This idea made his twin feel better. "Oh, the poor thing!" She giggled. "Let's go up this street and see if we can find it."

When they came to the corner Freddie said, "I'm going to shut my eyes. When I open them the station will be there!"

They both shut their eyes but opened them very fast when someone called, "Thank goodness, here you are! Why did you leave the station?" It was Mr. Bobbsey.

"Oh Daddy, dear Daddy," was all Flossie could say as she hugged him.

Freddie took his father's hand and walked beside him. He wanted to explain why they had left the station by themselves so that his father would understand that they had not meant to go so far.

"There was a boy with a goat hitched to a cart, Daddy," he began.

Flossie took up the story quickly. "The boy said he'd give me a ride in the cart. I wanted to go for a teensy-weensy ride. That's why Freddie had to come, too. He really didn't want to."

"I see," said Mr. Bobbsey, but added sternly, "Do you remember what you promised me about going alone on the streets of New York? The city is very big and you can get lost so easily."

"Yes, I know Daddy, and I'm terribly sorry," Flossie said, squeezing his hand. "But we knew you'd find us."

They had reached the station, which was just down the street, after all, and before long they were on their way to join the others at the Museum of Natural History. They found Mrs. Bobbsey waiting for them in the entrance hall.

"The twins and Jack are in Akeley Hall," she said. "They've seen the Roosevelt exhibits. Goodness, Flossie!" she broke off to exclaim. "What happened to your hair? You look as if you'd been in a cyclone!" She smoothed Flossie's curls and brushed the dust from her dress.

"I guess I almost was, Mother," Flossie replied with a giggle.

"Tell me about it later," Mrs. Bobbsey requested.

They went into the great Akeley Hall with its fine group of mammoth elephant figures in the center. Around the sides of the rooms were huge glass cases in which groups of stuffed wild animals looked as if they were nibbling food or sleeping or even playing. The scenes around them were built and painted to look like their native countries.

"Isn't this one lifelike?" Nan said as she paused to gaze at it.

The scene was of a river with distant blue hills. In the foreground zebras and giraffes grazed peacefully.

Freddie giggled. "I wish I had a neck like that giraffe. Then I could see everything in the parades and at games."

When the Bobbseys came from the hall, Flossie spied a group of figures in the big main foyer. "Who are these people?" she asked, running over to the glass case.

"The man with the wooden leg," said Mr. Bobbsey, "is Peter Stuyvesant, who bought the island of Manhattan from the Indians. The Indians are holding sprigs of tobacco in their hands to show that they are coming on a peaceful mission."

They went to the marine exhibit and then into the hall of the American Indians. The children liked the exhibits of the Central and South American as well as Mexican Indians, showing their crafts and customs.

"They sure don't live the way we do," Bert remarked to Nan. "They have more outside than inside their huts."

"They do most of their cooking outdoors," Nan said.

"Oh!" cried Freddie. "Look at the enormous peashooter that man has." The little boy was staring into a case where a Central American Indian held a very long blow gun to his lips.

"That doesn't shoot peas, Freddie. It shoots poisoned arrows," Jack Whittle told him. "This

card says that some of those men can strike a target with an arrow from more than thirty feet away."

"I s'pose the children practice on pea-shooters so they can use blow guns when they grow up," remarked Flossie as they left that exhibit and went to the great hall where carcasses of strange prehistoric animals stood.

"Wow!" exclaimed Freddie gazing up at the largest dinosaur. "I'm glad I wasn't alive when he was walking around!"

"So am I!" exclaimed Flossie. "He must have looked funny though without any skin."

Bert laughed. "He had skin then, Flossie. These are just his bones that were found millions of years after he died. The museum men put them together so we could see how big the old fellow was."

"Here is a dinosaur who left his footprints, Nan," Bert called. "How would you like to have found *these* tracks in the sand up at Lake Metoka?"

Nan ran to look at the ancient marks imprinted on the stone. "Imagine meeting one of those gigantic animals!" she cried.

Flossie had been standing near the door waiting for the rest of the family to finish looking at the exhibit. She was very hungry.

"Mother," she called, "when are we going to have lunch?"

"Soon, dear," Mrs. Bobbsey answered. "I know you must be starved. There's a good cafeteria in the basement of this building."

"I hope so," Bert exclaimed. "I'm so hungry I could eat an *eohippus!*"

Everyone laughed, for they had all seen the picture of that animal who was the early ancestor of the horse.

"I'll have a chance then to look at my mail," Mr. Bobbsey said as they went down the stairs. "The hotel clerk handed it to me just as we were leaving. I have a Lakeport paper too."

"Oh, here's a shop where we can get postcards," Nan cried. "I want one to send to Uncle Jack. He was so interested in this museum." She and the older boys went in while the others waited, but soon returned.

In the cafeteria Mr. Bobbsey held a table while the children and their mother filled trays for themselves and one for him. When they came back he looked up from the Lakeport paper and exclaimed:

"There was a burglary at the Meredith estate. It happened last Saturday. The big house was ransacked and a secret safe emptied. The house has been vacant, you know, since Mr. Meredith died."

"That man we saw in the Meredith woods— he must have been the burglar!" Nan cried.

"This sounds exciting," Jack exclaimed. "Tell me about it."

The twins gave him a detailed account of their meeting with the horrible looking man, the poster in the Lakeport station, and their seeing the fugitive in Pennsylvania Station upon their arrival in New York.

"What a tale!" Jack exclaimed. "And you think he's covering up his scarred mouth with a big mustache, but he can't disguise that drooping eyelid."

"I'm not convinced the man is in New York," Mr. Bobbsey said, smiling, "but I do think the twins may have seen the burglar in the woods on Saturday."

"It's about time for the Planetarium show," Mrs. Bobbsey said as they left the restaurant. "Let's go up now and find good seats for it."

"I hope the show won't take too long," her husband said. "I have to be down on Wall Street by five o'clock for a last meeting with those men from out of town."

"I'm sure the show will be over in time," Mrs. Bobbsey said.

Later, as the twins sat in the great darkened auditorium and watched the stars move over the dome-shaped ceiling which looked just like the sky, they forgot about the Meredith mystery. A man explained the different constellations.

"I feel as though I were out on a great plain under the stars," Nan whispered to Bert.

"I'm certainly going to study astronomy," he vowed in a whisper. "This is keen stuff."

As they came out into the sunlit outer hall Mr. Bobbsey said, "Come over this way. I want to weigh all of you." He walked toward some scales set against a wall.

"Do you know how heavy you are, Jack?" he asked.

"About a hundred and twenty pounds, sir," replied the tall boy.

"Let's see what you would weigh if you were on the Sun. Step on these scales." Mr. Bobbsey pointed to a small platform.

Jack did so and looked at the figures. "Zowie! That scale says three thousand three hundred forty-six and four-fifths pounds!" cried Jack, unable to believe his eyes.

"Wow!" exclaimed Bert. "You really fattened up in a hurry, Jack. Say, this one here is the Moon scale. How do you read it, Dad?" He stepped on.

Mr. Bobbsey bent to see the numbers. "How you've lost weight, Bert!" he said. "You were up to a hundred and five when we weighed you the other day. Now you are sixteen and four-fifths pounds."

"Help!" Bert laughed, hopping off. "I'll try my Sun weight next."

Flossie stepped onto the Venus scale and Freddie chose Mars. Nan tried to figure her weight on Jupiter.

Mrs. Bobbsey read the figures and laughed. "You'd certainly be a fat girl if you lived on Jupiter. You tip the scales at two hundred fifty and two-fifths pounds."

Nan jumped off quickly. "I'm glad I live on the Earth planet," she said, giggling.

Freddie weighed only twenty pounds on Mars instead of his normal fifty-five and Flossie's weight shrank to eight and a half pounds on the Venus scale.

"Why you're just a good-sized new baby!" her mother told her.

"Why are they all so different, Dad?" Bert asked.

"It's a matter of attraction, son. Your weight on each one varies according to the pull of gravity that each planet possesses," Mr. Bobbsey answered.

Flossie stifled a yawn. "Is there anything more to see, Daddy?" she asked.

"Not today, honey," he answered. "I see you've had about all you can take. You are going back to the hotel now with your mother."

As they left the museum Mr. Bobbsey turned to Bert and Nan who were walking with Jack. "Would you three like to go down to lower Manhattan with me? I think you'd enjoy that."

They accepted enthusiastically. Mr. Bobbsey added that the streets of the financial district were called the "canyons of New York." When Nan asked why, he said, "We'll go up to the top of one of the high buildings and you'll see why."

After a short ride Mrs. Bobbsey and the younger twins left the subway train to go to the hotel, but the other four continued on to lower Manhattan.

The train began to fill up as it was after four o'clock, and office workers were starting for home. Nan sat quietly watching the people, wondering where they lived and what they did. Suddenly she gripped Bert's arm.

"There he is!" she whispered. "Don't look yet. He's across the aisle about halfway down the car. Look now," she murmured presently.

Bert stole a glance in the direction Nan indicated. There sat the man with the brown mustache and on his tie was the clasp with the ruby-eyed horse. The man was looking the other way so Bert could not see his eyes, but in a minute he turned. The left eyelid drooped, nearly covering the eye.

Just then the train slowed to a stop and the man quickly left the car. Bert jumped up.

"Come on!" he called to the others in excitement. "We must follow that man!"

CHAPTER XI

MONKEYSHINES

BERT and Nan dashed out of the train so quickly that Mr. Bobbsey and Jack Whittle had to hurry to catch up with them. The twins pushed their way through the crowd on the platform.

"Hurry!" Bert exclaimed. "He went up those stairs!"

He and Nan raced toward the steps, with their bewildered father and Jack following. When Bert and Nan reached the street, they looked around for the burly figure wanted by the police—but he was nowhere in sight.

"Would you mind telling me whom you're chasing?" Mr. Bobbsey asked humorously as he and Jack came panting up the stairs.

"It was Dogface Pete, Dad," Nan told him eagerly. "I know it was."

"Well, I'm sorry you lost him." Their father

looked at his watch as he spoke. "My appointment is in twenty minutes. I'll notify the police, then we'll walk to the building. It's only about two blocks from here."

While he was gone, Bert and Nan surveyed the "canyons of New York." The streets in the financial district were narrow and the buildings very tall. Not much of the sky could be seen.

"I always think of canyons as being out West," Nan remarked. She giggled. "With horses and cowboys on them. These canyons are certainly different."

Jack laughed. "But the men here who buy and sell things that have to do with horses and cattle and grain and leather use some of the same expressions as cowboys do, like 'take your hide,' 'get roped in,' 'given a bad steer.' Sales to a lot of people are sometimes called a 'good round-up' and men in loud clothes are known as the 'cowboys of Wall Street.' They even say a restaurant is a 'chuck wagon!' "

The twins laughed. Soon Mr. Bobbsey returned and the group started off again. On the way to his appointment he pointed out the Stock Exchange and the Sub-Treasury building where George Washington had taken the oath as first president of the United States. As they stood looking up at the statue of the great man Bert remarked, "This really makes history come alive."

When Jack and the Bobbseys reached Mr. Hanks' office, he welcomed them warmly. "Sit here by the windows," he said to the children, pulling up some big chairs, "and admire the view while your father and I talk business."

"What do you suppose old Peter Stuyvesant would think of this?" Nan queried as they looked out.

"If I could say 'I don't believe it!' in Dutch I'd be able to tell you," Bert replied with a grin.

"I think I'll mail this card to Uncle Jack when we leave here," Nan said, drawing it from her pocket. "Do you want to see what I wrote?"

Bert took the card and read aloud: "This is a wonderful museum. We'll tell you about it when we get home. Was the man in the woods the burglar? Nan."

"I've written mine too," Bert said, handing over another card.

Nan read:

"Dear Uncle Jack:

We think the man we saw in the woods Saturday was the one who robbed the Meredith place. We told the police about him. I'm sure he's the same man as in the poster in the Lakeport station, D. F. Pete.

Bert."

As she handed the card back to Bert, Nan giggled. "It sounds as though the poster had a picture of a Mr. D. F. Pete!"

Bert grinned. "I know. I didn't have room to put his full nickname but I think the police will know which one it is."

Jack had been watching and listening. Now he said, "You Bobbsey twins have more excitement than any other four people I know."

"We do seem to collect adventures," Bert admitted.

Nan had been thinking. "Bert," she said, "I believe Daddy should write to the Lakeport police. These cards to Uncle Jack aren't enough."

Mr. Bobbsey's meeting was over shortly, and he and the three children took the subway back to the hotel. That evening, after Freddie and Flossie were asleep, Bert said to his father, "Dad, Nan and I think you should write the Lakeport police and tell them that we think the man we saw in the Meredith woods on Saturday is in New York."

"Yes, Dad," Nan urged. "And please tell them that we are sure he is Dogface Pete."

Mr. Bobbsey looked thoughtful. Then he said, "The New York police have probably already contacted our chief."

"But they didn't tell them Dogface was carrying two heavy suitcases when we saw him. I'll bet they held the loot from the Meredith safe!"

"It seems odd he would use the train," Mr. Bobbsey observed.

"Well Dad, if that was his old jalopy we saw in the woods he couldn't have gone very far in it," Bert reasoned.

Mrs. Bobbsey spoke up. "I agree that you should write Chief Smith, Richard. The twins are pretty good detectives and perhaps they're right about the man bringing the loot to New York."

"Very well," said Mr. Bobbsey, smiling. "That settles it. I'll write tonight. Now you two must go to bed. Remember we have a busy day tomorrow at the Bronx Zoo."

"Oh Dad, thank you. I'm so glad you're going to the zoo with us and that you asked Bruce and Jack, too," Nan said, giving her father a hug.

Promptly at nine the next morning there was a knock on the door of the Bobbseys' suite. When Bert answered he saw a short, smiling man with a shock of white hair standing there with Bruce. "Good morning," he said pleasantly. "You must be Bert. I'm Bruce's grandfather. I want to thank you for including him on your trip today."

Bert invited Mr. Dickerson to come in and introduced him to the family and to Jack Whittle, who had arrived a few minutes earlier.

Mr. Dickerson and Mr. Bobbsey talked for a few moments, then Bruce's grandfather said to the boy, "Bruce, you are to consider yourself a Bobbsey twin today and do just as Mr. and Mrs. Bobbsey say."

"Hooray!" shouted Bruce. "We'll be three twins, Flossie and Freddie and I."

After a low voiced conversation with Mr. and Mrs. Bobbsey, Mr. Dickerson went on his way. Soon they all were on the subway headed for the famous zoo located in Bronx Park.

"Oh!" cried Flossie when they came out of the tunnel. "This train goes upstairs too!"

She and Freddie knelt on the seat and stared out of the window. The streets and apartment houses whizzed by, and soon it was time to get off.

"I think it would be better to walk through the open air exhibits than to take the tractor train," Mrs. Bobbsey said.

"Yes," her husband agreed. "We can see much more. We'll take the train to come back to the gate when we're ready to go home."

The Bobbseys and Jack wandered along the lovely wooded paths past the replica of the African plains. Here zebra and antelopes nibbled at the grass, while cranes and great fluffy maribou storks stalked about stiff-legged under blossoming trees. A peacock spread his great beautiful tail and paraded before the admiring audience.

"Oh look!" cried Freddie, pointing to where, on a mound of flat topped rocks, lions were sitting or lying in the warm sunlight.

"What keeps them in? There's no cage or wire net at all!" cried Bruce. "Will they jump out?"

"They're very comfortable where they are," replied Mr. Bobbsey. "But at the base of those rocks, where you can't see it, is a deep moat which separates the lions from the rest of the African plain. It's too wide for them to jump over."

"That's good!" Flossie exclaimed. "What are those funny peaked things that look like straw houses, Daddy?"

"They're like the houses in some of the African villages, my little sweet fairy. How would you like to live in one?" he teased her.

"I like our house better, Daddy," the little girl answered with a giggle.

Next the visitors walked past the huge apes and gorillas in their outdoor homes and into the monkey house. A family of gibbon monkeys—mother, father, youngster, and a baby—were playing on the horizontal bars in one cage. Their antics were so like those of humans that the onlookers laughed as they watched them.

"See the baby!" Flossie cried in excitement.

The littlest monkey was clinging to its mother's back as she swung hand over hand along the topmost bar.

"It's enjoying a free ride," Nan observed, and the baby monkey did indeed look very happy.

It was hard to leave the monkeys, but Mrs. Bobbsey urged that they go on to the reptile house. There they saw an enormous tortoise egg which the twins' father said would provide breakfast all year for a whole family.

"Let's get a tortoise, Daddy," Freddie suggested. "Then we'd never have to buy eggs."

"I want to see the skinks," Nan said, "especially the stump-tailed one. I read in a book that he stores his food in his tail."

Bert had halted before a glass case. "Here's one," he called. "It looks just like a lizard. This one is named a blue-tongued skink."

Freddie pressed his nose against the case and tapped the glass. "I want to make him stick his tongue out!" he explained. When the animal only blinked sleepily, Freddie followed Bruce and Flossie down to the end of the room.

Nan found the stump-tailed skink and stopped to examine it. "He doesn't look very happy, even if he does have food in his tail," she mused.

Looking up, she saw the small children standing by a solid, low tile fence which surrounded a pool. On the wall back of the pool was a sign. In large black letters were the words:

ALLIGATORS! KEEP BACK!
DON'T PUT HANDS OVER WALL!
THE ALLIGATORS CAN JUMP!

Suddenly Nan saw Flossie lean over the tile fence and wave her hands above the pool!

CHAPTER XII

ANIMAL RIDES AT THE ZOO

WHEN Nan saw Flossie put her hands over the low wall of the alligator pool, she ran faster than she ever had before. In a flash she reached her sister and pulled the little girl back. Just as she did so, an alligator leaped into the air, snapping its jaws viciously.

"Oh Nan!" Flossie cried, clinging to her sister when she saw the ferocious looking reptile. "I was going to pat him!"

The two little boys stared aghast when they realized what might have happened to Flossie. "You're a real hero, Nan!" Freddie announced.

By this time Mr. and Mrs. Bobbsey and the two older boys had joined Nan and the others. When they heard the story, Mr. Bobbsey put an arm around Nan's shoulders. "That was quick thinking," he said. "We're proud of you!"

Flossie gave her sister a great hug. Smiling, Mrs. Bobbsey said, "Perhaps we'd better find a safer place. I suggest that Bruce, Freddie, and Flossie go to the Children's Zoo. Only small children are allowed in, so the rest of us will wait at the pony track while they go in by themselves."

"May I have a pony ride too?" Freddie asked.

"You all may. There are several kinds of other animals to ride, too," his father assured him.

The three smaller children ran down under the "low bridge" entrance to their own zoo. "I'll pay for you," Bruce announced. "Granddad gave me some money."

The animals inside were tame and loved to be petted. Three tiny pigs lived in a very cute little white house. When Flossie saw it, she made a face and remarked, "But their porch is awfully dirty!"

"Well, it's really a pig sty!" Bruce teased her.

When they went up to look into Noah's Ark, a card there asked them not to tell what they had seen inside the ark. Giggling over this secret they left the children's zoo and joined the others.

"Now I'm going to have a pony ride," Freddie said expectantly. "I'll choose that black one in the pony ring."

"I think I'll ride the camel," Bert announced. "Who else wants to come? There's room for four in that seat on its back."

"I'll ride with you, Bert," Flossie offered.

"I'd like to come, too," Bruce spoke up.

Nan had been watching the animals as they were led around the track, "I believe I'll take the llama," she said. "He looks so proud and he steps along so carefully."

"I was going to choose him," said Jack, "but my legs are too long. I'll go with the others on the camel. That will make the foursome."

The children climbed up on their strange mounts as Freddie went across to the pony ring. He pointed to the black pony as his choice.

The boy who guided the ponies said doubtfully, "He's been acting mean today. Wouldn't you rather take another one?"

Freddie looked at the black pony who was standing very quietly eating some grass. "I'd like the black one," he said firmly.

"Okay." The boy shrugged and helped the little boy to mount. "I'll lead him."

As soon as Freddie was on the pony's back trouble began. First the fiery little animal rushed off up the track, trying to break away from the boy who held him. When this did not succeed, he swerved suddenly to the side of the road and scraped Freddie's leg against the fence.

Freddie hung on tightly while the boy guide pulled and shouted at the bad little black pony.

It finally trotted rather unwillingly around the track, but Freddie had a long scratch on one leg from his contact with the fence.

"You'd better get that scratch fixed up, sonny," the boy guide said as he helped Freddie off the pony. "There's a First-aid Station across the way."

Mrs. Bobbsey had been watching Freddie's struggle with the black pony; and when he told her what the boy had said, she turned to her husband. "I'll take Freddie to the First-aid Station," she said. "We'll meet you at the entrance to the Lion House."

"All right," he agreed. "I'll wait for the other children. I think Nan was having a little trouble with her llama, but he seems to be under control now."

Just then the camel loped up, and the four riders climbed down. "That was fun!" Flossie cried. "It was sort of like being in a big rocking chair."

Jack laughed. "It was lucky we could get on while he was standing. My father and I rode on one once at a fair. We mounted while the camel was kneeling and we really got knocked around when he stood up!"

"Look at Nan!" Bert exclaimed. Glancing over, the others saw Bert's twin sitting very straight on the llama which was down on its knees. The keeper was yanking at the stubborn animal's reins. Finally, with a lurch which almost toppled Nan from her seat, the llama stood up.

"Good for Nan," Bert said admiringly. "She didn't let that beast throw her!"

"Congratulations," Jack said when she joined the others. "You're a good rider!" Nan looked pleased.

Mr. Bobbsey said Freddie and his mother would meet them. They were standing by the dignified stone lions at the entrance to the Lion House when the others arrived.

"Most of the animals are outdoors," Freddie announced. "But there're some fish inside."

They walked into the large room. One side was taken up by aquariums set into the wall. On the opposite side all but one of the cages were empty. The lions and tigers that lived in them were enjoying the outdoors.

In the last cage a large tiger lay stretched on a ledge. He stared calmly at Freddie who stood in front of the cage.

"I think I'd like to be a zoo keeper when I grow up," Freddie told Bruce who was standing beside him.

"I'd like to be the zoo lady who takes care of the baby animals," Flossie joined in.

"Come see the lung fish," Bert called to them.

"It can live buried in mud." The three children hurried over to look.

Suddenly an ear-splitting roar filled the room. The great tiger had leaped down from his ledge. Pacing back and forth close to the bars, he let out loud snarls of rage.

"He's angry that you left him," Bert teased Freddie.

"I guess I won't be a zoo keeper after all," Freddie said hastily. "Let's go!"

The group left the Lion House and walked past the outdoor cages where leopards, ocelots, black leopards, cheetahs, and lionesses prowled about restlessly. The lions were stretched out on their rocks in the African plains.

The Bobbseys stopped in front of the cheetah's cage. "I feel better acquainted with cheetahs than with the others," Bert remarked, grinning. "Hello, you up there! Is your name Rajah, too?"

The silent-stepping, tawny cat looked indifferent and bored. He gazed over Bert's head as if he did not see him.

"He's not very polite," Flossie observed. "Why doesn't he look at you when you speak to him?"

Nan was reading the card on the cage. "He's probably thinking about some of the exciting hunts he had when he was in India," she explained. "This identification card says cheetahs were tamed to be used in hunting big game."

"I don't think it's fair to train cheetahs to catch other wild animals," Freddie protested.

"Come on, children," Mr. Bobbsey called and led the way across the plaza toward the stairs to the lower level.

"Oh daddy," Flossie cried, "look at the pink birds! What are they?"

"Flamingoes. They're wading birds from the tropics. Aren't they pretty?"

In the pond, white swans mingled with the rose and flame-colored flamingoes. One of the pink birds stood on the grass looking very grumpy, all huddled into a flaming ball.

"He has just one leg!" Flossie exclaimed. "Oh, the poor thing! No wonder he looks sick."

At that moment one of the birds in the pond drew up its head which had been thrust deep into the water. It uttered a strange raucous call. Quickly the bird on the shore responded. Up went its head on the long neck and the second leg, which had been tucked under its body, came down. The bird stepped carefully into the water.

"Look! I'm a flamingo!" Freddie shouted as he tried to stand on one leg. He lost his balance and fell against Bruce. The two boys went down on the grass together, laughing hilariously.

"Maybe I'm too hungry. My stomach is

empty, so I'm not heavy enough to keep my balance," Freddie reasoned when he stood up.

"I see a good place to have lunch," Nan told her mother. "Over there. We can watch the birds and animals while we eat."

"That's called Flamingo Terrace Restaurant," Bert informed her. "I saw the sign. It's a cafeteria."

The sightseers walked over to the restaurant and chose a table under a large red and white striped umbrella near the flamingo pond. Nan offered to stay and hold the table while the others selected their food inside the building.

"Suppose Bert and I stay with you," Jack suggested. "There's a big crowd here. It may take three of us to hold the table."

"Right," Bert agreed.

The three children sat down, and the other Bobbseys went with Bruce into the restaurant.

"Most everybody's eating hamburgers or frankfurters," Freddie remarked. "May I have one of each, Mother?"

Mrs. Bobbsey smiled. "I think one will do," she said.

Presently Nan said to Bert and Jack, "I think the animals here are pretty lucky. They have a beautiful place as a home. They're fed the right food without having to hunt for it. The polar bears have icy pools to bathe in, and the African animals have their plain. They shouldn't look so unhappy and bored."

"But, Nan," Jack objected, "they want to be free to hunt their own food and find their own dens. How would you like to be caged and not free to go about as you wanted to?"

"I wouldn't like it at all, of course," Nan replied promptly. "But if these animals weren't brought here, we'd never be able to see how—"

Nan's sentence ended abruptly as she saw a flash of tawny color near the parapet by the lion house. The next second a large graceful object vaulted the parapet to the wooded section below, directly across from the Flamingo Terrace. As Nan watched, speechless, the animal left the brook where it had stopped to drink and came out from among the trees.

Just then someone shrieked, "A lion is loose! Run for your lives!"

CHAPTER XIII

AN AMUSING CAPTURE

AT THE cry that a lion was loose everyone on the terrace, except Nan and the two older boys, rushed for the restaurant building. Chairs and tables were overturned, women and children screamed, and men shouted.

"It's a cheetah!" Bert cried when he saw the spotted, tawny coat. "I know how to keep him busy till his keeper comes. Let's collect all the hot dogs and hamburgers from the plates and feed him."

He jumped up, grabbed a paper plate and began gathering the meat from the tables nearest to theirs. Nan and Jack quickly did the same.

As the cheetah stepped softly onto the terrace, Bert tossed the plateful of food in front of it. The animal paused and in an instant had gulped the meat. As the cheetah raised its head, Nan threw her plateful in front of it. Jack was ready

with another as soon as the second lot was gone.
Bert was back with more after that.

"We're running short," he whispered. "Do
you think you can get some from the restaurant,
Nan?"

His twin hurried to the door which was
opened just wide enough to admit her. People
crowded around.

"My goodness!" cried one woman. "You're
brave youngsters! Aren't you afraid of that
leopard?"

Mr. and Mrs. Bobbsey pushed through the
throng. "Oh Nan!" her mother cried. "I'm glad
you're all right. Where are the boys?"

"Mother, it's a cheetah and we're keeping him
busy eating until the keeper comes. Please, let
me get some more meat."

"I'll go with you," said Mr. Bobbsey.

The cook at the meat counter handed Nan a
basket of frankfurters and the girl slipped out
through the narrow opening in the doorway
with her father.

Bert met her and quickly threw half the contents of the basket to the cheetah. The food disappeared in a few seconds.

"Oh why doesn't the keeper come?" Nan worried. "Here, Bert, give some more!" She knew
that as soon as it was gone, she and the others
would have to race into the building.

The cheetah had finished and was looking at her.

Bert threw the last of the meat, saying, "This cheetah looks as tame as Rajah, but I wish it didn't eat so fast."

When the last bit of meat was gone, the cheetah moved slowly and gracefully toward Nan, who still held the empty basket. She set it on the ground and hastily backed away. As the animal searched for the last crumbs, the Bobbseys and Jack saw two men running down the steps of the lion house. One had a rope, the other a bundle.

The keepers reached the terrace while the cheetah was still exploring the bottom of the basket. Quickly, one man snapped a collar on the animal's neck. Bert told about feeding the cheetah.

"That's good," one of the men said, then added, "All right, Salah, I guess you won't need this meat we brought. You've had your dinner."

"You're mighty plucky folks," said the other man, who was holding the cheetah's collar. "This animal is tame, but you didn't know that. How come you were so calm and collected?"

"We had an experience with a cheetah just last week," Bert answered, "so we took a chance on feeding this one till you came."

"How did it get loose?" Nan asked.

"Salah is mighty smart. The patent lock evidently didn't fasten after I had been in the cage this noon to give medicine to her mate. She clawed it open."

By this time people had begun to come out of the restaurant. Among the first were Mrs. Bobbsey, Freddie, Flossie, and Bruce.

"Oh, you were so brave!" Flossie exclaimed to her sister and brother and Jack.

"Yes," their father agreed. "I'm very proud of you for the way you handled this situation."

The men from the zoo thanked the children for their help in capturing the cheetah and went off with Salah trotting meekly beside them.

Now that the danger was past, the crowd came back to the tables and fresh food was brought from the restaurant. Presently, a small car drove up to the Fountain Circle, and a man walked over to the terrace.

"Where are the Bobbsey twins and Jack Whittle?" he asked, looking around.

Quickly the crowd pointed them out. When the three stood up, the stranger walked over and shook their hands. "I am the zoo manager," he said, "and I want to thank you. You probably averted a panic in the park. I would like to give you a reward of some kind."

"Oh no, sir," Bert protested. "We don't want any reward!" Nan and Jack echoed him.

Freddie said in a loud whisper to his mother, "I want my lunch!"

Mrs. Bobbsey put her finger to her lips in an attempt to silence her small son. But the zoo manager had overheard the remark.

"Well now," he exclaimed, smiling, "I think the zoo should stand treat for all those whose lunches the cheetah ate!"

There was a burst of applause from the crowd. The man turned to Mr. Bobbsey and said in a low tone, "I'd really like to do something for these courageous youngsters. What shall it be?"

"I'm grateful to you for thinking of it, but our children don't do things for a reward. I'm sure the twins and Jack are happy to have been of help in a bad situation," Mr. Bobbsey replied.

"I understand," the man said, "and we're very grateful. At least I hope you'll all have a good lunch as the zoo's guests."

They thanked him, and he went on his way. Later when the party was once more seated at the table under the red and white umbrella, Flossie said thoughtfully, "I hope I'll be as brave as Nan and Bert and Jack when I grow up."

Bert laughed. "I'm sure you will. As a matter of fact, I think Jack was the bravest one today. He had never met a cheetah!"

"And was I scared!" Jack admitted with a grin. "But you and Nan were so cool and calm that I couldn't run away and leave you!"

It was three o'clock before the Bobbseys and their guests left the Flamingo Terrace. They walked over to see the bright-colored birds in a great cage nearby.

"I'd like to live where I could see birds like these every day," Flossie declared.

"Then you'd also see tropical snakes and alligators," her father said teasingly. "Would you like that?"

"Oh no," Flossie answered with a little shudder, remembering the reptile house. "I wouldn't like that a bit."

In a few minutes they came to the little trackless train which would take them back to the subway. Trailing behind the driver's cab were three open cars with seats across them.

Freddie, Flossie, and Bruce took a seat at the rear of the last car, while Bert, Nan, and Jack sat down in one of the front seats. Mr. and Mrs. Bobbsey chose a place in the middle of the car.

The little train started up and soon was rattling along at a fast pace. It bounced and jerked as the engine sped on its way.

"Whee!" cried the three on the back seat. "This is fun!"

Mr. Bobbsey turned to warn them to hold on

tightly. Just as he did, Freddie screamed, "Oh Daddy! Bruce fell out! Bruce fell out!"

"Stop the train!" Mr. Bobbsey called.

"Stop the train!" another passenger echoed.

The cars came to a jerky standstill. Mr. Bobbsey, Bert, and the driver got out and ran back up the road. They found Bruce seated on some dried leaves in the soft dirt, a surprised expression on his round face.

"Are you all right?" Mr. Bobbsey asked anxiously as he helped the little boy to his feet. "Do you hurt anywhere?"

"N-no," Bruce answered slowly. "I guess I'm just out of breath." The boy was trembling.

The driver patted him on the back. "I guess you're all right, sonny," he said. "But after this hold on tight when you're riding in the back car. It sways more than the others."

"What happened, Bruce?" Bert asked as they walked back to the train. "How did you fall out?"

"I reached for a branch as we went under it," Bruce told him. "Just then we went *whish* round a curve and I fell out!"

"I'll sit on the outside now," Flossie announced, but neither Bruce nor her twin would agree to that.

"You might fall out, Flossie," Freddie explained. "Girls should sit in the middle."

Flossie looked unconvinced but moved over to let Bruce have his old seat again.

"All aboard!" shouted the driver. "Hold on tight, everybody."

Off they went on their bumpy, jumpy ride back to the gate. When they stopped, the back-seat riders were the first ones out and running. They went toward the park entrance.

"Bruce seems to be all right," Mrs. Bobbsey said. "I was going to look him over for bad bruises, but he's too lively to be hurt."

After the Bobbseys and their friends were on the subway train, Mr. Bobbsey said, "We're going back by way of Grand Central Station. I want you twins to see it. This train goes right underneath it."

When they left the train, down deep underneath the ground, Freddie asked, "Are we under the big station now, Daddy?"

"Indeed we are, son," his father answered. "And now we're going up to the big waiting room."

"What a 'normous place!" Flossie exclaimed presently as they walked into the huge room.

At that moment a great voice boomed out somewhere above them:

MR. RICHARD BOBBSEY. PLEASE COME TO THE INFORMATION DESK.

CHAPTER XIV

A DISCOURAGING ERRAND

THE big voice that called Mr. Bobbsey's name seemed to come from the ceiling. The twins stopped short and looked all around them in amazement.

"Who is it that has such a loud voice and wants Daddy?" Flossie asked, standing close to her mother.

"Let's go to the information desk and find out," said Mr. Bobbsey. He did not look worried. He was actually chuckling.

He and the others went across the marble floor to the desk in the center of the room. Nearing it, they saw two familiar figures. Bruce ran forward crying out:

"Grandma! Granddaddy!"

Mr. and Mrs. Dickerson stepped up to greet the group. They were laughing.

"Mr. and Mrs. Bobbsey and we thought it

would be fun to surprise you," Mr. Dickerson said. "I knew you were to be here at five o'clock, so we were watching. I had you paged over the loudspeaker as soon as I saw you enter the waiting room."

"We sure were surprised," Bert said. "We wondered who would be paging Dad in New York."

"Mrs. Dickerson and I thought we'd take you all to dinner," Bruce's grandfather said. "Shall we have Italian, French, Chinese, Swedish, Syrian, Japanese, or a plain American dinner?"

"Goodness!" Flossie exclaimed. "Are they all different?"

"Indeed they are," Mr. Dickerson replied. "Well, who has a choice? Don't be shy!"

When no one spoke, Nan said hesitatingly, "I'd like to go to a French restaurant."

Bert spoke just a second after Nan. "Chinese for me." He stopped when he heard Nan.

Mr. Dickerson laughed. "French it is tonight, because Nan spoke first. Perhaps we can go down to Chinatown tomorrow evening."

"We'll walk up Fifth Avenue and enjoy the beautiful evening," Mrs. Dickerson suggested. "It's a little early for dinner."

"That would be lovely," Nan agreed. "I like to look in the wonderful shop windows and see all the tall buildings."

They walked slowly up Fifth Avenue, watching the homeward-bound people board buses. Then, after several blocks, Mr. Dickerson led the way around a corner and into an attractive restaurant. The walls were covered with autographed pictures of actors and actresses.

"This is fun!" Flossie squealed as the headwaiter led them to a large corner table.

Mr. Dickerson ordered a delicious dinner, and when they had finished eating it he said, "How about baked Alaska for dessert?"

"How can you bake Alaska?" Freddie asked with a puzzled look.

Mr. Dickerson laughed. "The Alaska part is ice cream," he explained.

Flossie spoke up. "But I don't see how you can bake ice cream. It would all melt!"

"Wait and see, little sweet fairy!" Mr. Bobbsey teased.

When the dessert was served, the children gasped in amazement. Baked ice cream! The outside was crusty and the inside cool, sweet ice cream.

"This is dreamy!" Nan exclaimed.

Later when Flossie was climbing into bed, she said sleepily, "Oh, Mother, this was such a fun day and it ended with hot and cold ice cream. I'm going to ask Dinah to make it for us."

The next morning the Bobbseys were up early,

ready for another active day. This one was to include a further hunt for the Whipples.

Bert called Jack on the telephone. "Remember we're going to Staten Island," he said. "We're leaving the hotel at about nine-thirty."

"I'll meet you downstairs. I wouldn't miss this trip for anything!"

Mr. Bobbsey was unable to go because of business, but Mrs. Bobbsey and the twins were at the door of the hotel promptly at nine-thirty. Jack was there before them. "Hi there!" he called. "I'm all ready for another Bobbsey adventure."

"And I hope we solve the mystery," Nan added.

The group took the subway down to the Battery once more, and Jack whispered to Bert, "Be sure to let me know if you see that man again."

"I'm watching out for him," Bert replied. "I'll give you a signal if I think I see him."

At the ferry house they stood in a big waiting room behind a gate until the boat was ready to load its passengers. When the gates opened, there were several people besides the Bobbsey party waiting to go aboard.

"This place is really crowded on a Sunday in the summer," Jack told them. "It's a favorite way for New Yorkers to get cool."

"I can see why," Nan said, sniffing the air, "I

smell the sea already, and there's a breeze."

As they walked onto the ferry, Flossie cried, "Oh, what a darling little dog!"

A small white terrier stood at one side anxiously watching each person who came aboard. When he saw Bert, he ran up to sniff his shoes. Then he went back again to take up his watch.

Flossie declared the dog had a worried look on his whiskered face. She stooped to pat his head. "The poor thing's lost his master somewhere on this boat," she said. "He must be a boy about your age, Bert."

When the ferry left the dock, the children made their way up to the forward deck, with Mrs. Bobbsey following. They all lined up along the rail.

"I'm glad we brought our sweaters," Nan said as she helped Flossie into hers.

"So am I!" Flossie agreed. "Oh, here's the little doggie again!"

The terrier had evidently not found his master. After sniffing around for a minute or two, he curled up under one of the seats at the side of the deck.

"Does that dog belong to a member of the crew?" Bert asked a man sweeping the deck.

"No. But he's been on the boat most of the morning," the man replied. "He seems to be looking for someone."

"What happens to the pup if no one claims him?" Nan asked.

The man shrugged his shoulders. "Who knows? Maybe the captain will take him home."

"I'll bet he's hungry," Bert remarked. "I'm going to get him a hamburger." He ran below to the refreshment stand and soon returned with a fat meat patty.

The little dog arose, wagged his stumpy tail, and took the hamburger from Bert's outstretched hand. Then as the bells clanged, and the ferry nosed into the slip, the stray animal stationed himself in view of the gang plank.

"Well, doggie, I hope your master comes aboard this trip," Bert said as they left the ferry. "Good luck!"

"Now," said Jack as they went through the big waiting room to the street, "we must look for the cobbler shop of Mr. David Whipple."

"I have the address," Bert added, fishing in his pocket. "Here it is. Well, believe it or not, this is the street."

"You three go ahead and interview Mr. Whipple," Mrs. Bobbsey told them. "Flossie and Freddie and I will stroll along and look at the town."

"Yes, perhaps it would be confusing to have us all barge into his shop to ask him questions," Bert said.

He and Nan and Jack hurried up the street and soon saw the cobbler's sign on a small building. A man was busy at a machine in the rear of the shop. As he came forward he asked, "What can I do for you?"

"We're looking for a Mr. David Whipple who has a brother named Jack," Bert said. "We saw your name in the telephone directory, so we came to see you."

The cobbler looked at him sharply. "Why?"

Nan answered this time. "We're hoping to find the brother of a dear friend who lost track of his family a long time ago. Do you have a brother Jack?"

"Yes, I do," answered Mr. Whipple, smiling, "but he's far from lost. He lives up in Maine with his wife and ten children."

"Our friend was born in Oregon and isn't married," Bert told the cobbler, "so it's plain that you aren't the same family. Thank you for giving us your time."

The twins and Jack went out to join Mrs. Bobbsey and the small twins. "Any luck?" Mrs. Bobbsey asked.

"No, Mother," Nan replied. "But we won't give up."

Flossie tugged at Bert's arm. "See that boy over there?" she asked. "He looks sad and he's been whistling and calling a dog. Do you s'pose he's looking for the one we saw on the ferry?"

"It could be," Bert answered. He crossed the street and said to the boy, "Have you lost a small white dog, by any chance?"

"Yes, I have! Did you see him?" was the eager reply.

"I think so," said Bert. "When we crossed on the ferry, there was a white terrier watching for someone. He stays on the boat, a man told us, and looks at all the people each time it docks."

"Hurray!" shouted the boy. "That's Tags all right. He came over with me early this morning and when we got here he took off after a cat. I've looked all over town for him. I never thought he'd go back on the ferry."

Nan giggled. "The cat must have run onto the boat. Then it started off."

"Well, thanks a million," the boy said.

He set off on a run for the dock and when the Bobbsey group came aboard a few minutes later they found him and his pet waiting on the boat.

"Now your dog's smiling," Flossie remarked, as the terrier thumped his tail and opened his mouth in a yawn.

The boy laughed. "I forgot to tell you my name. It's Ted Allen. What's yours?"

Bert introduced himself and the others. "I'm mighty glad you and Tags got together," he said.

Mrs. Bobbsey looked from one boy to the other. "I see why Tags ran up to Bert," she said. "You look somewhat alike, are about the same size, and your sweaters are almost identical."

"That's right," cried Ted. "No wonder Tags was mixed up."

The boys talked all the way across the bay about school, baseball, and various other activities. Bert told him about trying to find the Whipples. Ted said he had never heard of anybody with that name, but if he did, he would let the

Bobbseys know. Bert gave him his hotel and Lakeport addresses.

When the ferry docked, Ted said, "I might never have found Tags if it hadn't been for you. I hope I can help you some time."

That evening at six, Mr. and Mrs. Dickerson and Bruce called for the Bobbseys at their rooms.

"Jack and his father are going with us to Chinatown, too," Mrs. Dickerson told them. "We're to meet downstairs."

As Flossie put on her coat she sang:

"Here we go down
To lovely Chinatown!"

Mr. Dickerson laughed and said, "This is more fun than I've had in a long time. I'm so glad you Bobbseys came to New York!"

"So are we, sir," Bert told him, grinning.

The Dickersons' party crowded into two taxicabs and drove toward Canal Street through the bustling early evening traffic. After a long ride they came to a part of the city unlike any they had seen before. The streets were narrow and the buildings no more than three stories high. Some of the little shops bore signs in Chinese characters. Venerable old men sat outside smoking long pipes.

"We'll get out here and walk up and down Mott and Pell streets a bit before we go into the restaurant," Mr. Dickerson said, signaling the other cab to stop, too, and climbing out.

As the visitors strolled along, Mr. Bobbsey pointed out to the children items in the shop windows which they had neither seen nor heard of before. One store advertised dried sea horses, and its windows were filled with curious dishes of dried fish and bundles of faded herbs.

"Here is the restaurant," Mrs. Dickerson called finally, stopping before an ornate building with a curving red roof.

The others followed her inside and they were shown to a long table. Two smiling Chinese waiters came to serve them.

"Will you have birds' nest soup, Freddie?" Mr. Dickerson asked with a twinkle in his eye.

CHAPTER XV

FREDDIE thought he had not heard right. "B-birds' nest soup?" he asked.

Mr. Bobbsey laughed. "It's very good, Freddie."

"Well, maybe I'll try some with a little bird's egg in it," Freddie ventured.

"You're a good sport," Mr. Dickerson praised the small boy. "But I suggest that we skip it and just let the waiter bring us a good Chinese dinner." The others nodded assent.

The smiling waiters withdrew but soon returned and placed a small cup without handles and a pair of chopsticks at each place. One by one the children were shown how to hold the chopsticks. The Dickersons explained the cups were for tea.

While the group waited for the food to be served, the children practiced holding the chop-

142

sticks with one hand and trying to open and close them. The sticks kept falling to the table, and Flossie could not stop giggling.

Finally Freddie sighed and said, "I guess I'll have to eat with my fingers."

The first course after the soup was sweet and sour pork served on a large platter in the center of the table. A plate was given to each guest, who was to reach over and help himself. The Bobbsey twins waited for Mrs. Dickerson to start. How clever she was with her chopsticks!

"Oh dear," said Flossie presently when she was unable to carry any of the meat to her plate, "I'm afraid I'm going to starve."

A waiter standing nearby handed her and Freddie each a fork and the little twins looked relieved. They enjoyed the rest of the Chinese dinner.

The other children caught on quickly and thought it was fun to use the chopsticks. After the platter had been removed, another was brought in. On it were slices of roast duck with chunks of pineapple, and tender shoots of bamboo. A small bowl of rice was given to each of the Bobbseys and their friends.

"It's just as different as can be from the dinner we had last night," Nan observed, "but it's just as good."

"I'm glad," said Mrs. Dickerson. "But you've

hardly begun on this dinner. There are eleven courses."

"Eleven!" the children chorused and groaned.

"The Chinese say they can eat more if they drink a lot of tea," Mr. Dickerson said, laughing, and picked up his cup.

The visitors spent a long time over the meal and ate a little of each course. At the end Freddie sighed happily. "I'm stuffed," he said, "but thank you just the same, Mrs. Dickerson."

The others laughed and all expressed their thanks. "It was great!" said Bert.

By the time they left the restaurant it was dark. From nearby came the sound of music and laughter. Someone began to sing a lively tune in a deep, rich bass voice.

"Let's see what's going on!" Jack urged.

Mr. Dickerson agreed. "Yes. We mustn't miss anything."

As they walked toward the corner, the music grew louder. "It sounds like an accordion and a violin and some other instrument all playing at once," Nan remarked, "but they're not playing the same tune."

"It's my guess," her father said, "that the accordion is accompanying the man who is singing. The violin and cello are playing dance music. Anyway, they're having a grand time."

"It sounds very gay," Mrs. Bobbsey said. "I wonder what they're celebrating."

"I think that's an Italian song," Jack commented. "But we're in Chinatown."

Mr. Dickerson stopped and pointed toward the cross street which they were approaching. "At that corner Little Italy begins," he explained. "Chinatown ends here."

"It sounds like a lot of fun over in Italy." Bert grinned. "Let's go!"

"Officer!" Mr. Dickerson hailed a passing policeman. "What's going on?"

"They're celebrating the birthday of the patron saint of this block," the man explained. "They sure can put on a fiesta, can't they?"

"They certainly can," Mr. Bobbsey agreed, as they reached the corner and looked up the narrow street.

Brightly colored lanterns were strung from one side of the street to the other, and crowds of gaily dressed dancers whirled about beneath them. At the near side of the street, two men in Italian peasant costumes played accordions with all their might. A stout young man, who had evidently been the singer, mopped his face with a large red handkerchief.

On the opposite curb a man was playing a squeaky violin. Beside him a very fat gentleman played a cello. Their tune was a foot-tapping country dance.

"Daddy! The people are dancing right in the

middle of the street!" Freddie exclaimed. "What if a car should come?"

"I think they've closed the street to traffic tonight," Mrs. Dickerson said.

"I wish I could dance in the street," Flossie said. "It would be lots of fun."

Three small children who were hopping about to the music called to the twins and Bruce. "Come ona dance. Come ona dance!"

"Oh, Mother, may we?" Flossie begged. "Just a little?"

"I want to dance too," Bruce announced.

"Go ahead," said his grandfather. "You don't often go to a party like this."

Mrs. Bobbsey said "yes" too, and the three delighted youngsters soon were stamping and turning to the rhythm of the melody.

"See, the three little Italian children are showing ours a special dance," Mrs. Bobbsey pointed out. "Isn't that cute?"

"I'd like to learn that one myself," Jack remarked. "Perhaps Bruce will be able to teach it to me."

Some young girls and boys saw Nan and the two boys standing by watching and hailed them.

"Would you like to dance, too?" one of them called. "We'd be glad to have you join us."

"Shall we?" Jack asked the twins.

"Sure! Come on!" Bert replied eagerly.

"Okay," Jack said. "But find yourself a partner. Nan and I have this dance together."

"We've done folk dancing in school," Nan said. "It's a lot like this. I'm sure we can follow them."

Bert had started toward the dancers. Now he suddenly turned back. "I just saw Dogface!" he exclaimed in a low voice. "He went across the street in a hurry. I think he noticed us and wanted to get away quick! Come on, let's find out where he's going."

"Who?" Jack asked. He had not caught the name.

Bert and Nan did not answer. They were already crossing the street, dodging the dancers as they ran. Jack darted after them.

"There he is!" Bert pointed. "The man in the plaid shirt is Dogface!"

"You mean that's Dogface Pete?" Jack cried. "Oh boy! Am I glad I'm here! What do we do now?"

As he spoke, the man started rapidly up the street. While the children watched, he turned the corner.

"After him!" Bert urged.

Followed closely by Jack and Nan, he ran up the crowded sidewalk and around the corner.

"There he is!" Nan exclaimed. "Just dodging into that doorway. We'll find out where he hides.

Then we can tell the police," she added as they stopped in front of the building.

"Let's go in," Jack proposed. He opened the door, then fell back with a startled exclamation.

Nan and Bert jumped back too. As they did, a man with a black mustache burst from the doorway. But this was not Dogface Pete!

"Why you chasa me like this?" he demanded. "Whata you want with me?"

"We thought you were someone else," Bert apologized sheepishly. "We're awfully sorry to have bothered you."

The angry man waved Bert's apology aside. "Get out of here!" he shouted. "And don't come back!"

"We won't," Bert assured him as the three children turned and ran down the street.

When they had turned the corner, Jack stopped to lean against a building and laugh. "Wow!" he cried. "Here I was being the big hero going after Dogface Pete, and this fellow jumps right out at me and scares me out of my wits!"

His laughter was so contagious that Bert and Nan began to giggle too. In a second all three were laughing hilariously.

When they had calmed down a bit, Nan gasped, "That poor man, being chased to his house by the three of us!"

"And I still haven't seen Dogface Pete!" Jack lamented.

"Well, we'll still let you help us catch him if we see him," Bert assured his friend.

"Let's go back and dance now," Nan suggested. "I think we need some fun after that experience!"

The block party was still in full swing when the three children returned. They quickly joined in an Italian folk dance and were learning some new steps when Nan saw Mr. Bobbsey making his way through the crowd toward them.

"I'm looking for Freddie, Flossie, and Bruce," he explained. "Have you seen any of the three children? We can't find them anywhere!"

CHAPTER XVI

A KIDNAPED DOLL

"FREDDIE and Flossie missing?" Nan echoed her father. "And Bruce too? But we saw them just a few minutes ago. They were dancing."

"All three children seem to have disappeared," Mr. Bobbsey continued as Bert and Jack came up.

"We'll look for them," Bert said when he heard the news. "I'm sure they can't be far away."

"Incidentally," Mr. Bobbsey went on, "we saw you and Nan running across the street, with Jack close behind. You looked as though you were hot on a trail! What was it?"

Bert looked embarrassed but confessed, "It was a false alarm this time, Dad. We thought we saw Dogface Pete."

"Well, turn your detecting to finding Freddie and Flossie," Mr. Bobbsey said. "We've looked up and down both sides of this street already."

"Okay, Dad. We're off!"

Bert, Nan, and Jack made their separate ways among the dancers in the street. Nan called the twins' names but the crowd made so much noise that she could not make herself heard.

Bert asked several of the smaller children if they had seen the twins and Bruce. Most of them shook their heads. But one little girl motioned to him to wait, and ran off. She returned in a few minutes with two very fat, sleepy babies, one under each arm.

"These are twins," she told him proudly.

"Thank you," Bert said. "They're very nice. But the twins I'm looking for are my little brother and sister."

"Oh," said the little girl in a disappointed tone. "I'll take these back then." She ran off through the crowd.

Bert resumed his search and soon met Nan and Jack. Neither of them had found any trace of the missing children.

While the three stood trying to decide what to do next, a young girl named Rosa, with whom Bert had been dancing a few minutes before, hurried up to them.

"I heard that your brother and sister are missing," she said. "I have just thought of something! Perhaps I can find your little twins for you.

Come with me!" She started across the street, and the three children followed.

Rosa went in between two buildings and along a narrow, dark passageway. As the searchers came to the rear of the buildings they saw several houses on the other side of a large yard.

"Rosa," Nan said, "is this where you live?"

The Italian girl climbed the stairs which went up the outside of a tall, dark house. The only light was one high up on the top floor.

"This is the house of my aunt," Rosa explained, looking over her shoulder at Nan, who was following with Bert and Jack. "But your brother and sister were with my little sister and her cousins and they have disappeared, too. I think they might be here."

"I certainly hope so," Bert said.

Rosa stopped beside a door at the top of the stairs. She opened it quietly, and suddenly they heard peals of delighted laughter coming from inside.

"That's Freddie!" Bert cried. "We've found them."

The entrance hall was dark, but Flossie's giggle and a squeal from Bruce led the searching party quickly into the lighted room beyond.

There on the floor sat the missing children. Each one held a wriggling, squealing little puppy. From a box on the floor nearby the mother dog watched her babies anxiously.

"How darling!" Nan exclaimed as she ran to lift the last little animal from the box. She held it close to her and stroked its soft fur.

"Remember, Nan, we came to get the twins and Bruce," Bert said, grinning. "We'd better hurry back or Dad will think we're lost, too."

"I wish we could have one of these pups." Flossie sighed, looking hopefully at her sister.

Nan smiled. "It would be nice, but I don't think the puppy would like living in a hotel."

"I guess not," Flossie agreed reluctantly and returned the little dog she had been holding to the box.

After saying good-by to Rosa's sisters and cousins, the six children followed the Italian girl down the dark steps. They made their way back to the crowded street.

Nan introduced Rosa to the waiting Bobbseys and Dickersons. "Rosa guessed where Freddie and Flossie and Bruce were," she told them. "If it hadn't been for her, we'd never have found them."

They all thanked Rosa for her great help. Then Mr. Dickerson hailed two taxis for their return trip uptown. It was long after the younger children's bedtime, and they were nearly asleep when the party reached the hotel.

The next morning, breakfast for the twins was

served in Mr. and Mrs. Bobbsey's room. They had just finished when Bruce and his grandfather came to ask Flossie and Freddie to take a walk in Central Park with them. "We'll feed the swans in the lake," Mr. Dickerson said.

"That's a nice idea!" Flossie exclaimed. "And I'll take my dolly that Mr. John gave me. I haven't taken her anywhere for a walk. I've been too busy."

The park was full of babies and their mothers or nurses. Young children ran happily over the green grass as men and women watched them. On the lake the pure white swans glided serenely over the glassy surface and their reflections were very bright.

"It's like two swans swimming," Bruce said. "Only one's upside down."

There were ducks, too—brown ones with glistening green feathers on their necks. They were much more curious about their visitors than the swans were.

Mr. Dickerson sat down on a bench near the water and took a bag from his pocket. "Put your doll down, Flossie, and I'll give you some bread for the swans. Here, boys, there's some for you, too."

Flossie had seated herself on a rock close to the lake. She put the doll down, got up, and hurried to get her share of the bread.

Bruce stood on a broad stone near the water. "Here, Swanny, Swanny," he called in a high voice. "Shoo! Go away, you greedy duck." He waved a brown duck away from the bread.

Freddie walked to another spot along the rocks and crouched down. He threw a few crumbs onto the water and waited. Presently a graceful swan drifted over to look at the bread. Then she bent her long neck and daintily swallowed the pieces.

Flossie had been watching her twin. Now she exclaimed, "I'm coming over there, Freddie!" and scrambled across the stones. She sat down beside her brother.

A little distance away Bruce was still calling, "Here, Swanny, Swanny!" Then suddenly he shouted, "Drop that! Go away!"

"What's the matter?" Freddie called.

"The duck! He took Flossie's doll!"

Flossie screamed and ran as fast as she could, but before she could reach the place the brown duck was swimming away. Grasped firmly in its strong bill was the doll!

"Oh, save my dolly!" Flossie wailed, bursting into tears.

"I'm afraid it's too late," said Mr. Dickerson who had come up to see if there was anything he could do. "I'm afraid your dolly is gone, but don't cry. She'll have a lovely home here in the park. Not many dollies have the chance to live on a lake."

Flossie looked at him through her tears. "But she'll have a duck for a mother," the little girl sobbed, "and I don't think she'll like that."

"I'm sure the duck will be a good mother," Mr. Dickerson consoled her. "Now, I have a plan. We'll go back to the hotel and get Nan and Bert and Mrs. Dickerson. Then we'll go to my store and find another doll for you, maybe even a better one. All right?"

Flossie thought for a moment, then a smile broke through her tears.

"After we get the doll, we'll go up to the top floor and see a camp exhibit. Then we'll have lunch together. How would you like that?"

Freddie and Bruce jumped for joy. Quickly they all went back across the park to tell the others of the plan.

Meanwhile, the other Bobbseys had received some exciting news. Shortly after Freddie and Flossie had left for Central Park, Nan and Bert had gone down to talk to the registration clerk.

"Good morning," said the young man at the desk, "I have some mail here for your father and mother. Would you mind taking it up?"

"Not at all," Bert said as the clerk handed him the bundle, then he added, "By any chance, was David Whipple registered here lately?"

The clerk looked thoughtful. "That name does sound familiar, but he's not one of our guests now."

The twins waited anxiously for the man to recall more, but after a moment he shook his head. "If I remember, I'll let you know."

"Thanks a lot."

Bert and Nan left him still looking puzzled and went up to their suite.

"Dad, here's mail for you." Bert handed

the bundle to his father. "There's a Lakeport paper too. May Nan and I glance at it to see if there's anything new on the Meredith robbery?"

"Of course, son," Mr. Bobbsey replied. "The chief of police must have my letter now."

He and Mrs. Bobbsey were reading their letters when Bert jumped up crying excitedly, "Dad! Mother! Listen to this!" He read:

"A new development in the Meredith robbery has upheld the theory that it was an inside job. Yesterday the police found a small brown satchel under the porch of the caretaker's cottage. In it were a few jewels and several valuable papers that had evidently been taken from the private safe in the Meredith mansion.

"The caretaker, Jack Whipple, has been under suspicion from the first, because the location of the safe would not have been known to an ordinary thief. Mr. Whipple has now been placed under arrest on burglary charges, but is at present out on bail."

"How awful!" Nan exclaimed.

"Dad! We must do something quick," Bert stormed. "Dogface Pete was carrying a satchel when we saw him in the woods, and I think Snap heard him when he was prowling around Uncle Jack's house."

At that moment the telephone rang sharply.

"Maybe it's something about the mystery!" Bert cried as he ran to answer it.

CHAPTER XVII

WORRISOME NEWS

"HELLO," Bert called, picking up the telephone. "This is Bert Bobbsey speaking."

"Good morning, Bert," a voice answered. "Chief Smith of the Lakeport police here. I just received a letter from your father saying that you think you have seen this Dogface Pete in New York. Is that right?"

"Oh yes, sir," Bert replied eagerly. "I'm glad you called. We just read in the Lakeport paper that you found a small brown satchel under Mr. Whipple's cottage."

"We certainly did," the chief said.

"The man we saw in the woods was carrying a bag which sounds like that," Bert continued.

"Mm. Very interesting," Chief Smith commented. "But now tell me about the man in New York that you think is Dogface Pete."

Bert took a deep breath, then started in. "Well, we noticed the man in the Meredith woods was wearing a tie clasp with a horse's head on it. Then we saw Dogface's picture in the post office, and he looked just like the man in the woods. My sister saw the man with the horsy tie clasp get on the train in Lakeport and we saw him the next morning in the station here. He's wearing a false mustache."

"Thanks very much, Bert," the officer said. "I'll get in touch with the New York police and put them on his trail."

"But Chief, we've already told the New York police. They're looking for him."

"Very good. And now put your dad on the wire, Bert."

While Mr. Bobbsey was talking, Jack Whittle came in.

"Good news!" Bert cried. "The Lakeport police are on the trail of Dogface Pete at last. But they've got the wrong man. Look at this article in the paper."

He showed Jack the account of the caretaker's arrest for robbery. "That's terrible!" Jack exclaimed. "I hope you'll be able to clear him. I'm going down to tell Dad about your Uncle Jack's arrest. He's a lawyer and maybe he can help your friend."

As Jack went out, Flossie and Freddie ran into the room. "Nan! Bert! Bruce's grandfather is taking us to his store to—" Freddie began.

". . . to get me a new dolly," Flossie broke in. "A nasty old duck stole my Joan, so he said he'd give me another and we're going—"

"Whoa!" Mr. Dickerson called, following the little twins into the room. "Let me give this invitation. Mrs. Dickerson, Bruce, and I are asking the Bobbsey twins and their parents to lunch with us at the store. We have a camp exhibit which I think you'd enjoy seeing."

"That's very kind of you," Mrs. Bobbsey said. "Mr. Bobbsey and I have a luncheon engagement, but I'm sure the children will be delighted to go with you."

"It'll be great!" Bert exclaimed. "I'm keen on camping!"

Nan was just as enthusiastic about the invitation as her brother. "How wonderful!" she cried. "I've been wanting to go into one of the big New York stores, but we haven't had time since coming to the city."

"Good!" said Mr. Dickerson. "I'll go collect my wife and Bruce, and we'll meet you in about twenty minutes."

"We'll be at the elevators," Bert suggested.

When Mr. Bobbsey finished his phone call, Freddie and Flossie told about their adventure in the park with the swans and the greedy duck. Flossie's eyes filled with tears again as she thought of her lost doll.

"Perhaps the duck will put her back on a rock," Nan said comfortingly. "Some little girl will find her."

This thought made Flossie feel more cheerful and soon she was chattering happily as they drove through the New York streets in Mr. Dickerson's car.

When they entered the store, Flossie exclaimed, "It's bee-yoo-ti-ful!"

Nan also exclaimed in admiration. The large first floor was brightly lighted and the showcases and counters were filled with attractive merchandise.

"We'll start at the top where the camping exhibit is and work down," Mr. Dickerson suggested. "Is that all right?"

"Yes, sir," Bert spoke up. "I'd like to see the camp things."

When the group stepped from the elevator on the top floor, it seemed as if they had walked into a forest. There were real trees around, and the far wall was painted to represent a mountain lake. In the foreground a tent had been set up. Two men were crouched over a camp stove cooking their breakfast with the latest and best in camping equipment.

"They ought to be making flapjacks and flipping them into that long-handled pan," Bert observed.

Mrs. Dickerson laughed. "I haven't thought of flapjacks for years," she said. "Do you remember, dear, how proud I was of the ones I made when we were first married?"

"Indeed I do," her husband agreed. "They were delicious, too!"

Mr. Dickerson turned to one of the men in the camp exhibit and asked if he knew how to make flapjacks. The camper said he did.

"This young man here has a good idea," the store owner said, indicating Bert. "We'll have you make them while the exhibit is on. I think our customers would enjoy seeing you flip them."

The man agreed, and said he would start the next day.

"Now," said Mr. Dickerson, turning to Flossie, "we have some important shopping to do." The little girl took his hand as they went to the elevator.

The toy floor was pure delight to the children. One end was devoted to mechanical toys, and here little trains rushed along the tracks, signal lights flashing. A miniature airplane soared through the air. On the floor a mechanical satellite moved ceaselessly about among the standing displays.

Next to this was a room furnished as a doll house. Dolls of all sizes and in all sorts of costumes were seated in chairs and lined up on tables and counters.

"Flossie," Mr. Dickerson instructed, "look around and pick the one you like best."

The little girl inspected the dazzling array very carefully. There was one doll in a pink and white checked dress. She had yellow curls tied with a pink bow and little pink lace gloves on her tiny hands.

"I'm 'fraid that one is too 'spensive," Flossie whispered to Nan.

Mr. Dickerson had noticed that Flossie kept looking at the doll in the pink and white dress, so presently he took that one from the counter.

"I like this best," he told Flossie. "Would you please me and take her home with you?"

Flossie's beaming face was his reward. She clasped the lovely doll in her arms. "I think you are the nicest man in the whole world next to my daddy," she said as she thanked Bruce's grandfather.

"Now, Freddie, you and Bruce each find something you'd like. I want the Bobbsey twins to have a souvenir of this day. Bert, how about a model jet plane with a motor?" Mr. Dickerson asked.

"That would be neat, sir," Bert answered. "But I think you've done too much for us already."

"Nonsense. It's my pleasure," Bruce's grandfather replied briskly as he went with them toward the games section. Quickly he looked over the collection of planes. "How about this one?" he asked, showing Bert a box filled with pieces and a sheet of directions. He smiled when he saw Bert's delight. "Good! I'll wager you can beat your friends flying this memento of your New York visit."

Freddie and Bruce had been closely examining the display of miniature autos. Finally each boy picked a red fire chief's car.

"I want to get Nan's gift," Mrs. Dickerson announced. "It's on the first floor, so let's have lunch now and we can stop for that later."

They all agreed and soon were seated at a large

window table in the store restaurant. It was at the top of the building, and the children were entranced by the view of the skyscrapers. They were almost too excited to think of food.

"What will you have, Freddie?" Mrs. Dickerson asked after all the others had ordered.

Freddie thought for a moment. Then remembering the camp exhibit and Uncle Jack's supper, he cried, "I'll have some flapjacks!"

Mrs. Dickerson laughed. "I don't believe they're on the menu, but I'm sure you can have some pancakes. They're very similar."

"Freddie loves pancakes," Nan said with a meaningful look at her little brother.

He felt disappointed but replied politely, "Yes, pancakes will be fine."

When Freddie's order of pancakes was placed before him, it looked very small. His appetite had grown, thinking about the flapjacks at Uncle Jack's house, and he had looked forward to eating the pancakes. This plate of four very thin cakes was not much like the hearty plump flapjacks he had eaten at the cabin in the Meredith woods.

"More flap jims, Jack Jim," he said with a mischievous grin at Bert.

Mrs. Dickerson put down her fork suddenly. "What did you say, Freddie?" she asked, leaning toward him.

The little boy was embarrassed and, as his face grew red, Bert answered for him, "He's quoting something."

Nan put her hand on Bert's arm. She had seen an expression on Mrs. Dickerson's face which gave her a sudden brilliant thought. She, too, leaned forward. "Mrs. Dickerson," she asked, "could you possibly be Mr. Jack Whipple's sister Dodie?"

CHAPTER XVIII

TWINS FIND TWINS

AT NAN'S question Mrs. Dickerson turned pale. She stared at the girl without a word. Then slowly she spoke. "Yes, I am, Nan. But how could you know that?"

"From Uncle Jack," Nan replied excitedly.

"Wowie!" Bert exclaimed. "You do look like the picture!"

"Oh, oh, oh, we've found her!" Flossie cried. "We've found one of Uncle Jack's twins!"

Freddie jumped up and began hopping around the table until Nan pulled him back into his chair.

"This is amazing!" Mr. Dickerson commented. "I've heard about this wonderful brother of my wife's for years but I never expected to see him. Where did you know him and how is he your uncle?"

When everyone had quieted down the twins

said Mr. Whipple was not really their uncle. Then they took turns telling the Dickersons about their meeting with the caretaker of the Meredith estate and about his new troubles.

When they finished Mrs. Dickerson's eyes were wet.

"Poor Jack!" she murmured. "I must see him. And I must call David in California and tell him this wonderful news!"

"We'll go to Lakeport at once," her husband said, patting her hand. "If it's really your brother Jack, I'll certainly help him."

"It must be Jack," Mrs. Dickerson said. "No one else would know about the 'flap jims, Jack Jim.' I can't wait to see him."

"We were going home tomorrow," Bert spoke up. "But perhaps we could all get reservations for tonight instead."

"Fine. But before we leave the store I want to get something nice for Nan," said Mrs. Dickerson. "This *is* a very special occasion."

They left the dining room and went to the first floor. Mrs. Dickerson took Nan's arm and led the way to the jewelry counter.

"Let me see the gold bracelets, please," she said to the young woman behind the counter. When the tray of gleaming circlets was set before Nan, she was too overcome to choose one. Mrs. Dickerson took a beautiful but very simple gold bracelet and slipped it on Nan's wrist.

"There," she said, "that's suitable for a young girl. If you like it, I shall have it engraved with your name on the under side and with my initials to express my gratitude."

"I love it!" exclaimed Nan. "Oh, millions of thanks, Mrs. Dickerson."

The bracelet was left for marking and the excited group hurried out to the car. The twins were so excited on the way home that they could hardly sit still. "Wait till Jack hears we've found David Whipple," Bert chuckled. "Remember all those telephone calls we made!"

When they went into the hotel Jack Whittle was in the lobby. Bert and Nan hurried over to tell him the great news. "Say, that's great!" the older boy exclaimed. "You Bobbseys are some detectives! Imagine David Whipple being Mrs. Dickerson's brother!"

As they walked toward the elevator, the registration clerk called Bert over to the desk. "I remember now why the name David Whipple was familiar," he said. "He has been here to visit his sister Mrs. Dickerson. He lives in California."

Bert could not help laughing. "Thank you," he said. "I just found that out!"

The Dickersons went to the Bobbseys' suite to hear the rest of the story about Dogface Pete, and how their brother was being blamed for the robbery.

Mr. and Mrs. Bobbsey had returned from their luncheon and were surprised to see the others so soon. Flossie rushed to show her new doll as she shouted, "We found Uncle Jack's twins!"

Explanations followed, and Mr. and Mrs. Bobbsey were even more amazed than the twins had been. "What a coincidence!" Mr. Bobbsey exclaimed. "It's almost unbelievable."

"We have looked everywhere for Jack," Mrs. Dickerson said. "We've followed every clue without success. I never thought that he would come East, but we have advertised in all the papers at different times. He was a wonderful brother to us!"

"He looked for you, too," Bert told her. "He walked all over the West after he was fifteen, but the family who took you didn't leave any address when they moved."

Mr. Bobbsey went to the telephone and called the head porter's desk. "See if you can get nine seats on a plane for Lakeport tonight," he said. "If you can, please cancel my reservations on the train for tomorrow. If you can't get them, see if you can get nine reservations for the sleeper to Lakeport tonight."

"You two and Bruce must be our guests in

Lakeport," Mrs. Bobbsey said to Mrs. Dickerson.

"Hurray! Now I can see your fire engine, Freddie," Bruce shouted.

"That'll be swell!" Freddie answered. "I'll take you all around to see my friends, too."

"How happy Uncle Jack is going to be!" Nan said. "Now, if the police would only find Dogface Pete and clear Uncle Jack's name!"

A heavy knock at the door startled them. Mr. Bobbsey opened it to two police officers. "We want to speak to Nan and Bert Bobbsey," one of them said as they stepped inside.

The older twins went forward. "I'm Bert and this is Nan, my twin."

The men nodded and one said, "We've had a couple of phone calls from your dad and one from the Lakeport police that you children think you've seen Dogface Pete, or Peter Rocco, in New York and that you also saw him in your home town at the time of a robbery. Is that right?"

"Yes sir," Bert said. "And we know that he was the robber. When we saw him in the Meredith woods he was carrying that little satchel that the Lakeport police found under the caretaker's house. Mr. Jack Whipple is a friend of ours, and we know that he is not a thief."

"Well, would you two come with us now and

identify this man in our Rogues' Gallery? That's where we keep criminals' pictures. We want to make sure that you really saw Dogface Pete."

The others had left the room so that the policemen could talk to the twins in private. Now Nan went to tell her mother that she and Bert were going with the officers to the police station.

"The hotel guests will think we're under arrest," Bert said to Nan with a grin as they went through the lobby with the officers of the law.

Nan giggled as she saw the surprised expressions on some of the faces around them. "I don't care, if we can find the real thief," she told her twin. "Anything to clear Uncle Jack of these charges."

The police car went rapidly down into lower Manhattan to the building where the Rogues' Gallery of pictures was kept. There Nan and Bert were shown a bewildering number of photographs before they spotted the now familiar, ugly face of Dogface Pete!

"There he is!" they both cried at once.

The officer grinned. "I guess you saw him, all right," he said. "That's all we wanted to know. I'll have the car take you back at once."

When the twins returned to the hotel they found their mother packing hastily. "We have seats on the plane which leaves at six o'clock," she told them. "We'll have to hurry!"

When Nan went to her room to pack she found Flossie there playing with her new doll. "I think Mrs. Dickerson would like to see that picture of Uncle Jack that you bought, Nan," Flossie said.

"Oh, Flossie, why didn't I think of that!" Nan cried. She took the wrapping from the portrait and ran down the hall to the Dickerson apartment. Elsie opened the door for her.

Mrs. Dickerson came quickly to see Nan, who held out the picture. She studied it carefully. "Yes, that's our Jack," she said softly. "This looks just like a picture I have of our father. Thank you, Nan, for bringing it to show me. I can't wait to see him again!"

As Nan returned to their rooms she met Jack

Whittle just outside. "Bert tells me you are all leaving tonight," he said. "I came to say good-by and tell you my dad says he'll be glad to help Uncle Jack if he needs him."

"Thanks a lot," said Nan. "Come in. Did Bert tell you that we went with a police escort to the Rogues' Gallery?"

"Yes, and I saw you just as you climbed into the police car." Jack laughed. "Some one nearby said 'Look at that! And so young, too.'"

"Jack, you're fooling!" cried Nan. She knew he was teasing her.

Bert put one hand on Jack's shoulder affectionately. "It's been swell knowing you, Jack," he said. "You have helped make our stay here lots more fun."

Jack laughed. "What would I have done in New York without the Bobbsey twins?" he told them. "Please write and keep me posted on the rest of the mystery. I never did see Dogface Pete."

"I'll do that," Bert promised.

The Lakeport plane was nearly ready to leave when the Bobbseys and Dickersons reached the airport, and soon they were skimming over the ground before the take off. Freddie and Bruce sat together and Flossie was in front of them with Nan.

"Here we go!" squealed Freddie as the plane

rose into the air. "Oh, see New York way down there!"

The city looked beautiful in the soft afternoon light, and the Bobbseys watched until it faded away in the distance. The stewardess came then with their dinner, and they turned their thoughts to food.

All three of the little children were asleep when the plane came down at Lakeport. Sam was there to meet them, for Mr. Bobbsey had called home to tell Dinah and Sam of the change of plans and to expect guests.

"How's Snap, Sam?" asked Bert as they climbed into the station wagon.

Sam laughed. "He's jest fine now. He chased that old black cat that's been prowlin' round till I reckon it won't never come back."

"Uncle Jack fixed Snap when that bad man hurt him," Flossie murmured sleepily. "Just like a doctor."

Mrs. Dickerson smiled. "Jack always loved animals. Dear Jack!"

Early the next morning the telephone rang and Bert answered it. "Yes sir, we'll be ready," Nan heard him say. Her twin hung up, then told her, "Police Chief Smith wants you and me to go to the Meredith place and show him where we saw the thief."

"I saw him, too," Freddie said. "I ought to go with you."

"We're going to his house this morning so Mrs. Dickerson can see her brother," Mr. Bobbsey told him. "You come with us, and we'll meet Bert and Nan there."

Shortly after that, Mr. and Mrs. Bobbsey with the Dickersons and the three younger children drove away. Nan and Bert waited for the police car, which came in a few minutes. When they reached the Meredith estate, Chief Smith asked:

"Now which gate did you twins drive through?"

Bert pointed it out and they drove in.

"This is the road," said Nan. "But it looks different today, because the sun is shining."

They drove slowly along the rough wooded road until they came to a curve. There, just beyond, was the deep hole which the Bobbsey car had hit.

Bert got out and looked about. "I don't see where that other car could have gone," he said. "It just disappeared and there isn't any other turn." He walked back along the road peering on either side. "Look here!" he shouted. "The underbrush is broken as though a car had been driven into the bushes."

The police came to inspect it. "That's what happened!" said one.

"Oh here come Mother and Dad and the others!" cried Nan.

The Bobbsey station wagon was traveling

slowly along the unused road toward them. It stopped, and the younger twins popped out and came running up. Bruce followed them.

"Uncle Jack is Bruce's great uncle!" Freddie announced importantly. "But he's our uncle."

The policemen were coming back out of the broken underbrush, and Mr. Bobbsey went to meet them. Flossie wandered off into the brush at the side of the road.

"Look what I found!" she cried presently and ran out, holding a battered aluminum pie plate.

"Dinah's best pie plate!" Nan exclaimed.

"The thief *did* steal our blueberry pie then!" cried Freddie excitedly.

"And that was a blueberry stain on his face, not a permanent mark," Bert added, "just as Nan said it was."

"The man went into those bushes near the hole," Mr. Bobbsey said to the chief. "Bert, can you show the officer just where?"

Bert went quickly to a tall clump of shrubbery and disappeared behind it. After a moment he came out with a paper in his hand. "I found something, too," he said, handing it to the chief.

"I'll say you did!" exclaimed the officer.

They gathered around to look at the dirty envelope which he held. On one side was drawn a crude house plan. "That," said Chief Smith, "is a plan of the Meredith mansion's first floor."

On the other side of the envelope a name was scrawled. "Pete Rocco, General Delivery, New York City," it said.

"He dropped that out of his pocket when he hid from you," the chief concluded. "It's a wonder he didn't look for it."

"It was raining very hard," Nan told him. "Maybe he couldn't remember which bushes he hid in."

"I think Snap may have scared him away, too," Bert remarked. "Well, anyway, Uncle Jack is cleared. You know now who is the burglar."

"I guess we do, son, but we must wait until tho New York police catch Rocco," the officer replied. "Mr. Whipple will be freed very soon."

They all went toward the Bobbsey station wagon. "Where's Uncle Jack?" Nan asked.

"He's talking over old times with his sister," Mrs. Bobbsey told them. "It was a wonderful reunion! They are at his cottage, but we are taking him back with us in a few moments."

When Mr. Bobbsey and the twins told her about their discoveries which would prove Uncle Jack's innocence, she was as pleased and excited as they were.

"We'll have a celebration tonight," she cried.

Uncle Jack was a very happy man when he came to the Bobbseys' home that day. "Hurray for the Bobbsey twins!" he cried. "See what they accomplished in one week's visit to New York! It has taken my sister and me almost a lifetime of searching, and with no result."

Before the Bobbseys had been home an hour, Chief Smith called to say that Dogface Pete had been caught in New York and had confessed to the robbery and that Uncle Jack was free.

Mrs. Dickerson put in a call to their brother in California, and both she and Uncle Jack talked to him. He said that he would fly to New York the next day to see his long lost brother.

"Jack is coming back with us for a visit," Mrs. Dickerson told him. "But he says that he must return to Lakeport. The county has asked him to be superintendent of the new park which Mr. Meredith left to the public."

The news of this appointment had come shortly before the Bobbseys had reached Uncle Jack's cottage that morning. He told them that a man from the county office had come to express their confidence in his innocence and to ask him to take charge of the new park.

"I'm glad you're coming back," Nan said.

"So am I, Nan. Now I have a dear adopted family of twins as well as my own brother and sister. I am a very rich man and I have the Bobbseys to thank for everything."

"It's lucky," Freddie exclaimed, "that we went to the big city of New York!"